KU-072-865

bestselling author whose books have been translated into forty languages. He is a personal development specialist who trained in humanities at NLP University in Santa Cruz. He lives in France.

**Sandra Smith** was born and raised in New York City. As an undergraduate, she spent one year studying at the Sorbonne and fell in love with Paris. Smith taught French Literature and Language at Robinson College, University of Cambridge for many years and has been a guest lecturer and professor at Columbia University, Harvard and Sarah Lawrence College.

# ALICE ASKS THE BIG QUESTIONS

## LAURENT GOUNELLE

*Translated from the French by Sandra Smith*

corsair

CORSAIR

First published in Great Britain in 2020 by Corsair
First published in the US in 2020 by Little, Brown and Company

1 3 5 7 9 10 8 6 4 2

Originally published in France by Éditions Kero as
*Et tu trouveras le trésor qui dort en toi*, October 2016

A CIP catalogue record for this book
is available from the British Library.

ISBN: 978-1-4721-5356-2

Printed and bound in Great Britain by Clays Ltd, Elcograf S.p.A.

Papers used by Corsair are from well-managed forests
and other responsible sources.

Corsair
An imprint of
Little, Brown Book Group
Carmelite House
50 Victoria Embankment
London EC4Y 0DZ

An Hachette UK Company
www.hachette.co.uk

www.littlebrown.co.uk

*To my sister, Sophie*

Narrow is the way which leadeth unto life,
and few there be that find it.

—Matthew 7:14

# Part I

Do not conform to the pattern of this world,
but be transformed by the
renewing of your mind.

—Paul's Epistle to the Romans, 12:2

# 1

ALICE COULDN'T RESIST A WIDE SMILE OF SATISFACTION AS SHE put down the phone. The potential client from Qatar had short-listed the PR consulting firm she worked for. The call for bids had been discreetly announced six months before. The Qatar International Promotion Agency was looking for a partner in the West to boost the country's image, so people would forget their suspicions about Qatar having financed ISIS.

There were only five companies on the short list: two American, one Spanish, one German, and one French. One chance in five to get the contract. Alice was convinced they'd win.

She breathed in deeply and stretched out, leaning against the back of her chair, letting it pivot toward the large window of her office, where her image was reflected. She was an energetic woman wearing a simple fitted suit that contrasted with her mass of chestnut hair, which fell in rather messy, long curls. She switched off the light on her desk and her reflection vanished.

On the fifty-third floor of the Montparnasse Tower, you felt as though you were suspended in midair, in a darkening, late afternoon sky where several wispy clouds floated by. Down below, the lights of the lively, bustling city—a city where millions of people lived—were beginning to glow in the thousands of buildings that stretched out as far as the eye could see. Just now, when the offices were closing, the roads were crammed full of cars, and the sidewalks held swarms of little, insignificant figures walking slowly by. Alice smiled as she watched the crowds. So many people to influence, challenges to meet, so much excitement to feel. Since she had started attending the staff development seminars by Toby Collins, she was becoming more confident and finding more satisfaction at work despite the stressful, competitive atmosphere.

She breathed in again and relaxed. Théo was at home with his nanny by now. Paul would get home late, as he did every day. She might already be asleep by the time he was dropped off in front of their building. What would the taxis do at night if the lawyers didn't leave their offices so late?

*Can't wait for summer,* she thought. She wanted them all to be together. If her team won the Qatar International contract, she'd get a raise—that much was certain. Or a big bonus. How could they refuse her one? With that money, she could treat her family to an expensive holiday. Why not Australia, even? Australia—a dream from her youth, not yet realized.

The telephone rang. Her father.

"I'm at the office, Papa."

"Are you coming to Cluny this weekend, *chérie*?"

"Yes, of course."

"That's good news! Will Paul come as well?"

"If he doesn't have too much work, like making the rounds to see clients in prison. And if he agrees to skip his drawing class on Saturday. It's his only passion apart from prisons."

4

"Send him my best," he said, laughing. "Listen, I ran into Jeremy this morning. He doesn't look well at all. His mother is worried—she talks to me about him all the time. If you come this weekend, she'd really like you to make some time to see him."

Jeremy looking unhappy? Strange that she hadn't noticed it the last weekend she was in Burgundy. Jeremy, with his slender physique, dark blond hair, very light blue eyes, and delicate, soft features that revealed his great kindness. She remembered their childhood together in Cluny, their high-speed races in the ruins of the abbey, the fun they'd had daring each other, always with the same prize: a peck on the cheek on New Year's Eve. Their wild laughter in the middle of the vineyards during the harvest, when they hid to eat the grapes instead of picking them. Their first kiss on the lips when they were nine years old—she was the one who had kissed him—and how he had started to blush like Uncle Edouard's tomatoes. They had dreamed of traveling to the other end of the world together, to the place where they walk upside down, to Australia. Australia, even back then.

Poor Jeremy. She was very sad to learn he wasn't doing well. Everyone had been surprised by his radical decision after he'd finished college with such apparent ease. To give everything up like that, with his master's in Ecology and Sustainable Development in hand, and completely change direction.

Jeremy had been there for her when she had lost first her mother, then her best friend a few years ago, before she'd met Paul. Mourning had caused a profound crisis in her. He had listened to her with the patience of an angel, given affectionate support, and been truly helpful.

She wanted to help him now too, do something for him. But what?

She breathed in deeply while watching the crowd down below. Her profession was crisis PR, not psychotherapy.

The heavy courtyard door groaned on its hinges, making it hard to open. Jeremy slipped through and let it close by itself. It made a sound like the dull thud of a prison door. He took the narrow Rue Notre-Dame to the right, breathing in the cool air of the beautiful March day. Beneath his feet, the paving stones took on a golden russet color in the sunlight.

At the corner of the Rue Saint-Odile, nothing moved in the austere Treasury Building with its barred windows. Opposite, at the Tabac des Arts, a good dozen or so people were waiting in line to buy lottery tickets. First they paid taxes to the government, then they happily threw their money away.

Jeremy continued down the narrow street until he reached the Rue Lamartine, the main street of Cluny, a pretty little town with pastel facades and colorful storefronts. He counted thirty-six customers having coffee outside La Nation café. *Coffee,* he thought, *keeps the spirit awake, but without actually awakening it.* A little farther on, outside the second tobacco shop, fourteen people stood in line waiting to buy lottery tickets, ready to gamble on luck to improve their lives.

Jeremy counted twenty-two customers at Dupaquier, the upmarket specialty food shop. The delicious smells that wafted outside were enough to convert any vegetarian. And at least ten people were having some cheese and a glass of wine at the Panier Voyageur.

He turned around and headed back up the street. Low in the sky, the sun highlighted the carved stone jambs, pilasters, and other elements of Romanesque architecture. There were also a lot of people at Wolff's, the excellent optician, trying to improve their eyesight. But would they be able to see their own lives more clearly?

Thirty-four people sat at tables outside Germain, the pastry and chocolate shop, whose reputation extended far beyond the Beaujolais hills. Jeremy smiled. *People,* he thought, *they give in to their love of food when their souls seek only to satisfy their bodies.*

He turned off to the right along the Rue Municipale and headed toward the abbey, passing the Café du Centre with its belle époque décor, where he counted twenty-eight customers scattered around the outside seating area and the dining room. The wine lovers were even more numerous at the Cellier de l'Abbaye. When he reached the Place de l'Abbaye, he walked past the Brasserie du Nord, which was full to bursting— at least seventy customers—then continued up the Rue du 11-Août-1944, the Rue Mercière, and the Rue de la Barre. The travel agency promised its clients the chance to explore foreign lands, which made Jeremy smile.

Across the street, there were also a lot of people at the other wine bar, DiVINE Pleasure. A funny play on words for drinks that alter our consciousness without ever managing to raise it.

A few yards farther along, the street opened out onto the square in front of the sunlit church. Several parishioners were chatting outside. Jeremy greeted them as he walked by, then pushed open the button-tufted door. It closed behind him with the muffled sound of a bellows as he entered the cold space.

The smell of damp stones and the faint scent of incense wafted throughout the somber interior. Jeremy crossed the nave through a side aisle that led to the choir. His footsteps never broke the silence that reigned supreme in the church. He slipped into the vestry and waited in the semidarkness. The bells rang out, and he listened to their chimes until the final one, which echoed for a long time beneath the tall stone vaults. Then he slowly made his way to the altar and stood facing the congregation. The columns stood in a magisterial row, soaring upward toward

7

the ribbed vaults, and met in enormous Gothic arches that ran all along the nave, drawing the eye and the spirit toward the heavens. Everything in the church seemed immense, and this impression gave a feeling of tremendous open space in the solemn atmosphere. The side aisles and even the central section of the nave were rather dark, but if you raised your eyes, you could see the light, a brilliant light that inundated the vaults with almost supernatural clarity.

Jeremy looked down at his flock.

Twelve.

Twelve people were sitting there, scattered throughout the first rows.

He began to say Mass.

# 2

AFTER MASS, JEREMY ACCOMPANIED HIS PARISHIONERS OUTSIDE.
The sun glistened on the uneven old paving stones and illuminated the medieval facades of the small square.

Two quite elderly women stood around him, discussing
how to organize their charitable works. Victor, the retired
winemaker, walked over to him and handed him a little
jewelry box.

"Here, Father. I'd like you to have this."

Known by everyone in Cluny as the "Lord of the Manor,"
Victor was recognizable from a distance because of his somewhat
old-fashioned yet imposing appearance: the herringbone tweed
jacket he always wore, his confident features and wild white hair,
just like Karajan's. Now partly deaf, he compensated for this
weakness with an air of authority that couldn't hide his natural
generosity, along with a portliness that allowed him to take up a
lot of space despite his average height.

Jeremy opened the box.

"A watch?"

"Don't read anything into it! I simply noticed that you didn't have one."

"But it's a very beautiful watch."

"What?"

Despite his stutter, Victor's friend Étienne came to the rescue. Slim and quite short, he had soft features, snow-white hair combed over to one side, and an extremely kind expression in his eyes. The unlikely friendship between a deaf man and one who stuttered was less ridiculous than it might have seemed: Étienne's handicap, very noticeable in private conversations, lessened slightly when he was obliged to shout so Victor could hear him.

"The Father is saying...that it is v-very beautiful!" he shouted in his friend's ear.

"It's French, made in Franche-Comté. One of the last ones."

Étienne was a former employee at Victor's vineyard. The years had eroded the hierarchical distance between them, and since his retirement, he and Victor had become close. Sometimes a mere trifle led the Lord of the Manor to blow up and unleash his anger on Étienne, but that just made Étienne laugh. He was quite skilled at putting his former boss's outbursts into perspective. They had passed the torch to the next generation: Victor's eldest daughter had gone into business with Étienne's son. In their parents' day, the wine was a bit acidic—the gossips said they didn't keep the barrels clean—but it had sold well at a time when the French still drank table wine. Today, that wine wouldn't sell. The children had worked very hard to improve it and had succeeded. It was now greatly praised in the area, but its reputation barely stretched beyond Mâcon.

"That's very kind of you," said Jeremy, speaking loudly so he would be heard.

"I got it at Pradille, on the Rue Mercière, one of the last watchmakers who know how to take apart the movement to repair it."

"Hello, Father," Germaine and Cornélie said, virtually in unison.

These two little old ladies were known for their malicious gossip, and everyone in the town called the busybodies "overly zealous." Germaine had bright eyes, dyed black hair, and a rather large and somewhat hooked nose. She had a fondness for long, dark velvet culottes, which she wore with ankle socks as white as the roots of her hair. As for Cornélie, both her self-effacing personality and her appearance made her fade into the background: hair dyed a dull yellowish brown, beige cardigan, long pleated beige skirt, and beige leather loafers with tassels. She sometimes allowed herself a touch of whimsy: a green velvet headband.

Jeremy greeted them, then excused himself and went back into the church. He crossed the nave while glancing at all the empty pews. Once inside the vestry, he took off his chasuble and stole. The sound of muted footsteps and a slight rustling of fabric caught his attention. It was one of the nuns who lived in a wing of the rectory. He walked over to her and handed her the jewelry box.

"Sell it," he said, "and give the money to the poor."

The nun took it and smiled.

He thought about the Curé of Ars: In the nineteenth century, he had also donated to charity a watch he had received as a gift. When the person who had given it to him heard this, he presented him with another one, then another, until he understood that the priest would never keep one for himself. So he

11

decided to lend the priest one, and at last had the satisfaction of seeing him wear it. Jeremy often considered the Curé of Ars his spiritual guide.

Jeremy started up the spiral staircase to the bell tower, climbing until he was just above the belfry, in the little open space beneath the dome. He often went there to be alone, to step back and get some air.

He sat down on the ledge. The cool air had the lovely scent of trees and nature. Here he could enjoy the view down over the rooftops of Cluny. The roofs were covered in old tiles whose colors reminded him of the dark red peel of passion fruit. There were flat tiles and rounded ones that brought to mind the ones found in the south, their red contrasting with the brilliant blue of the sky. From up here, he could see as far as the tree-covered hills that surrounded the medieval city.

Twelve people.

He was young. He had his whole life ahead of him, and had dedicated himself to saying Mass for...twelve people. He took in a long breath. He had once imagined himself as someone who could guide people on the path to self-awareness, nurture them spiritually, lead them to joy. Twelve people. He immediately reproached himself for that thought: Was it not pride that led him to lament this way? Had he not dreamed of attracting a great circle of the faithful? He shook his head. No, his sincerity was real, his motivation pure, devoid of any self-interest—a true vocation. But how could he accomplish his vocation with a nonexistent flock? Twelve parishioners, mainly the elderly, half of whom came out of habit and the rest out of a kind of fearful superstition as they neared death.

Jeremy watched a bird as it flew along the rooftops, then disappeared behind the abbey bell tower, which stood tall, outlined against the blue sky. Or, rather, what remained of the abbey.

It had been almost completely destroyed during the French Revolution and had been used as a stone quarry by the villagers. To think that it was once one of the holiest sites in Christianity, with a religious order that had ruled over twelve hundred abbeys and priories throughout Europe and ten thousand monks. The power of his abbey had been considerable, directly linked to the Holy See, and several popes had actually come from Cluny. What remained of it today? Twelve believers lost in a church built to accommodate four hundred.

He took another deep breath of clean air. He could see, very far below, tiny people walking down the busy main street and adjacent alleyways. He watched them for a long time, thinking of all the souls he would like to help awaken, if only they would come to him. But for that to happen, their consciences would have to be jolted. They would need to sense that something existed apart from money and ordinary pleasures: shopping, video games, sex, and TV. Was that really still possible? He had the impression that he was one of the last representatives of a religion that was fading away. His motivation was flagging, and his feeling of uselessness in this respect weighed heavily on him.

He sometimes thought about his visit to the coal mine, when he was still doing his master's in Ecology. The director didn't understand that he was defending a type of energy from the past. He continued as if nothing had happened, talking about his work as if he didn't realize he had fewer and fewer customers, fewer and fewer workers, and that in the long run, his mine was condemned to disappear. Jeremy had felt sorry for him. But today, he wondered whether he was in the same situation. Except that coal was bad for people. The mine made them go down into the bowels of the earth, and when they came back in the evening, they were covered in black dust. The mine's closing was perhaps a sign of some positive development. But spirituality

13

elevated people, raised them toward the heavens. If spirituality disappeared, what would be left?

Jeremy sighed. He felt powerless, discouraged, helpless. And yet, in a certain way, he accepted his depression. Somewhere, deep within him, he could sense it: it was from the darkest shadows that light shone through.

# 3

THE ELEVATOR DOORS CLOSED WITH A GUST OF AIR ON THE downstairs neighbor who had just gotten on. She was blond, with a very polished, ultra-sophisticated appearance. Furious, Alice held her little boy's hand tightly and stared at the numbers that lit up as the elevator continued downward. Why had her husband smiled like that at the slut? It was easy to look beautiful when you didn't have a child to take care of and could spend half your salary on clothes and an hour and a half every morning on your makeup. And her husband fell into the trap. Infuriating.

The doors opened on the ground floor. The Barbie doll pivoted on her high heels and got out, her little Gucci bag slung over her shoulder. Alice dragged her son and her small, plain suitcase to the taxi stand. Paul followed, a travel bag in one hand and his cell phone in the other, reading his emails or the news as he walked.

Two hours later, in front of her father's house in Cluny,

they parked the car they'd rented at the Mâcon train station. A large eighteenth-century residence with tall, white mullioned windows, shutters painted a light Provençal green, and a pretty facade washed in pale pink lime and covered in wisteria. Théo got excited and ran ahead to ring the bell. His grandfather opened the door, and the little boy rushed inside, darting between his legs.

"The swings in the backyard are more interesting than me," the old man said, laughing. "Did you have a good trip?"

Alice kissed her father. Paul shook his hand. Every time she visited, she was happy to see her father so serene in spite of his advanced age. He had very fine white hair and a radiant face, with little wrinkles that spread out around his blue eyes.

They found Jeremy's mother, Madeleine, inside, holding a cup of tea. They said hello, and Paul disappeared upstairs with the bags.

"I'm not staying," said Madeleine, standing up. "I'll leave you to your family get-together."

"No, do stay!" said Alice.

"I don't want to burden you with my problems. I've told your father how concerned I am about Jeremy. I'm quite worried about him, you know." She started walking to the door.

"Papa mentioned something about it to me."

Once she reached the doorway, the old woman turned and looked at Alice. She had a sad, dreamy smile on her face. "To think he was torn between his love for God and his love for you. But he did idolize you as if you were a goddess! If only he had chosen you, he wouldn't be where he is today."

Alice, stunned, watched her walk away.

"Are you having some tea, *chérie*?" her father called out from the living room.

"Coming."

Everything was spinning around in her mind. She did, in fact, have a vague memory of Jeremy trying to seduce her years before, though rather awkwardly. She hadn't played with his feelings, hadn't led him on. Their friendship meant a great deal to her, but their relationship would remain at that. He hadn't reacted badly, hadn't shown any emotion in particular, and their friendship had, in fact, continued as if nothing had happened. She'd decided it was just a fleeting attraction at an age when it's easy to believe you're in love with people you socialize with. She found it hard to take in that he might have been so infatuated with her. When did that happen? Perhaps before he went into the seminary.

Alice anxiously bit her lip.

She thought back to the personal tragedy she'd lived through shortly afterward and the period when she was in mourning. Jeremy had supported her, listened to her, helped her as though nothing had happened, despite the fact that his love had been rejected.

"Here you are, *chérie*. Here's your tea."

"Thanks, Papa."

Alice automatically brought the cup to her lips and burned her tongue. Blind, that's what she had been. Blind to Jeremy's past feelings and now blind to his depression. She had seen him regularly during her weekends in Cluny, without ever noticing a thing. Her professional life had pulled her away from her closest friends.

She suddenly felt egotistical. Her heart aching, she thought back to the warmth Jeremy had shown to her husband. He was a saint, that Jeremy. She owed it to herself to help him, now that he was the one who needed her. She had to do something, anything, to make him feel better. He deserved it. And she owed him at least that much.

17

"Where are you taking me?" Jeremy asked, laughing. "I'm not in the habit of being kidnapped when I come out of the rectory!"

The little red Peugeot she'd rented sped away from Cluny along the local roads.

"To Chapaize. To the Saint Martin restaurant."

"We're going to Chapaize just to have lunch?"

"It's fine, it's only fifteen minutes away—not the other end of the world. We'll have more privacy than in Cluny, where everyone knows you."

"Is your family joining us?"

Alice shook her head. "Paul is taking it easy at the house. He's teaching Théo to draw."

A few minutes later, the little car was crossing the rolling countryside, its vineyards crowned with tree-covered hills. Alice rolled down her window. The wonderfully scented air filled the car.

They parked at the entrance to the sleepy village, which they walked through before sitting down in the sunshine at one of the small outdoor tables of the Saint Martin. They were right opposite the Romanesque church, with its magnificent square bell tower raised toward the sky. Chapaize was a very authentic historical village. Many of its old stone houses were washed with a traditional soft-toned lime, often adorned with sheltered passageways and dovecotes, and covered in wisteria and trumpet vine.

"Do you come here a lot?" asked Jeremy.

"Fairly often, yes. I love this restaurant!"

They ordered and the waiter brought them the white burgundy they'd chosen as an aperitif.

She raised her glass. "To the sin of gluttony we are about to commit this lunchtime!"

They clinked glasses, and she took a sip.

"Mmm, divine. Better than the wine at Mass, I assume?"

Jeremy just smiled.

They both fell silent.

"I ran into your mother."

No reaction.

"She's . . . worried about you."

"Mothers always worry."

Silence.

On the other side of the narrow street, the church bell tolled once, and the sound echoed for a long time, slowly fading until it was heard no more. A great tranquility reigned in the village and the feeling that time was standing still. It was the end of March, and there was a chill in the air, but the bright sunshine gently warmed their faces, just as it warmed the pale stones of the bell tower.

She waited in silence for a long time, then dived in.

"I'm also worried about you."

"Everything's fine," he replied, a little too quickly.

Alice made a face.

"Jeremy, you don't have to be a shrink to see that something's wrong."

At first he said nothing, but Alice knew how to get him to confide in her. He finally told her how unhappy he was, his loss of motivation due to his laughable number of parishioners, which completely undermined his mission and made him feel useless. He also confided his impression that Christ's messages were not being heard, that his own parishioners did not truly put them into practice in their daily lives.

Alice let him talk. All she could do was commiserate with

his frustration. Would anyone be able to continue carrying out a mission whose usefulness seemed so improbable?

When he had finished unburdening himself, silence fell once more, and nothing in the serene environment disturbed it. The church opposite seemed sleepy, even though it was bathed in bright sunlight.

"I can help you," said Alice. "If you give me free rein, I'll completely overhaul your marketing strategy. That's my profession."

"My *marketing* strategy?!!" He had nearly choked on the words.

"Those aren't dirty words, you know."

"We're talking about a church, Alice, not a business. And I have nothing to sell."

"I just want to study how you talk to people and see how you might adapt to their expectations, that's all."

"Their expectations?" he replied, somewhat distant.

"Listen, there is surely a way to do something, to manage to move these people by trying something different."

Jeremy raised one eyebrow and smiled sadly. "I'm touched by your kindness, but how could you hope to help me in a field that you know nothing about? You're not even a believer."

Alice grimaced.

"No problem," she lied. "I'm used to working in fields that are unfamiliar to me. That's what my profession is all about. I just have to get a handle on it. Piece of cake."

Seeing him look rather dubious, she added: "Do you think I'm an expert on lasagna? Chocolate spreads? Cars? No. But that didn't stop me from being a consultant to Findus over the scandal about using horsemeat in their lasagna, or to Ferrero about the chemicals in their Nutella, or to Volkswagen over their emissions scandal."

"Thanks for adding me to your list of hopeless cases."

Alice forced herself to smile, then picked up her glass and took a long drink as she watched Jeremy.

"In any case," he continued, "the examples you've given are all problems that resulted from the sale of products. That's something concrete, tangible. I don't think you're qualified when it comes to the spirit. The spiritual has nothing to do with the material."

Alice felt unbelievably annoyed. Who did he think she was? Only good enough to deal with Nutella?

She was so proud of her title as a PR consultant, respected in her field. She was a negotiator who was about to land an enormous international contract. Every day she devised strategies that affected thousands of customers.

"Remind me: how many people come to your church?"

He shrugged as a sign of his hopelessness. "There's nothing that can be done. It's a lost cause. Forget it."

She felt like a little girl who thinks she can swim across a lake and is told she is just being silly.

The last time someone had warned her that she would fail, she had just started at the company as an intern and had dared to come up with proposals while she was supposed to simply take minutes of the meetings. She had been gently put in her place: Her proposals wouldn't work. The client wouldn't like them. She had insisted, certain of the value of her ideas, and had fought for the right to present them. Not only had the client used them but their implementation had been a great success. Her internship had been transformed into a permanent contract.

*I don't think you're qualified when it comes to the spirit.*

Hard to swallow.

"Give me two months, and I'll find a way to double your congregation!"

He looked up. "I don't see how you could do that. And anyway, going from twelve to twenty-four won't change very much, you know."

She looked him straight in the eye. "A hundred! You agree

21

to follow my advice, and I'll get a hundred people to your church!"

He sighed sadly. "You're crazy, Alice. It's impossible. You are completely deluding yourself. This isn't the world of business. What you do in your company won't work in church."

The more he doubted what she said, the more she felt a furious desire to demonstrate her skills.

"I bet you I can do it."

"I don't even know where you would start, how your advice could work."

"It's too soon to say. But I'll find a way—that's my job."

He didn't reply.

"Will you take the bet?"

"With what I get in the collection box, what do you want me to bet?"

She gave him her most beautiful smile. "A kiss on the cheek on New Year's Eve!"

He smiled nostalgically, then finally whispered, "Okay."

She poured him some more wine and they clinked glasses.

She took a sip, savoring the satisfaction of having convinced him. Now she would have to roll up her sleeves and get to work. She started to wonder how she would go about it.

It was a new field for her, and the challenge was enormous, as Jeremy had reckoned. But that wasn't the main problem.

How could she admit it to him?

She took another sip of her drink.

Not only was she an atheist, a confirmed atheist, but she was also particularly allergic to anything that had to do with religion, horrified by religious knickknacks of any kind, and very ill at ease whenever she set foot in a church.

# 4

Okay, first she had to get a handle on the book, find out exactly what it talked about. But still, she wasn't about to leaf through it on the bus, or while waiting at the hairdresser's or the dentist's, even less likely at the office. Reading a client's company brochure or press clippings, no problem. But really, pulling out the Bible, just like that, in public, would be bizarre. She'd feel a little embarrassed.

Then she found the perfect "cover": by scanning the actual cover of the book Paul left lying around the house every evening, then using trial and error to adjust the format, she printed a book jacket that was the ideal camouflage.

And so it was that the following Monday evening at the office, having stayed until seven to look as though she had work to do (even though there wasn't much going on), she took the book out of her bag. It was bright red, with the title *Civil Code* printed in large white letters on the front and a small extract from article

716 highlighted in one corner: "When someone finds treasure on his own land, it is his property." Inside, as well, the illusion was perfect: the same ultra-fine pages, the same columns of text in a small font. You had to really immerse yourself in the book to discover the scam: the *Law* was replacing the *laws*.

An hour later, half slouched over her desk, absorbed in her reading, Alice was nervously biting her lip, on the edge of despair. If she hadn't given herself the task of helping Jeremy, she would have laughed—that's how grotesque she found the text. Pathetic, asinine, without a beginning or an end. Precepts that were inapplicable, when they weren't quite simply absurd.

How the hell was she going to be able to keep her word?

*Blessed are you when people insult you,* said Jesus.

Sure, let's see. Getting insulted is happiness, right? We dream about it every day.

*Happy are the poor in spirit.*

Now, that one was true: what's the point of wearing yourself out in the lecture halls at university until you're twenty-five to open your mind when all you need to be happy is not to have one! And besides, it's a well-known fact: without it, no one takes advantage of your credulity, no one tries to use you, no one makes fun of you ...

*If anyone slaps you on the right cheek, turn to them the other cheek also.*

*Of course. Why didn't that occur to me sooner?* she thought.

24

*And those who exalt themselves will be humbled.*

Well, well, that sounds like the latest educational reform.

*It is hard for someone who is rich to enter the kingdom of heaven.*

*Another reason to get rich,* Alice thought. *I'm in no hurry to get to heaven!* So, to sum it all up, to be happy, you have to be an idiot, get insulted, let people walk all over you, humble yourself, and become poor again. That's quite a curriculum.

*Before Abraham was born, I am!*

*Before Abraham was born . . . I am???* Oh boy. Grammar and verb tenses were obviously not his thing.

*One new humanity out of the two . . .*

Neither was math.

*That all of them may be one, Father, just as you are in me, and I am in you.*

Sounds like the mutual, incestuous insemination of hermaphroditic snails.

*When you unclothe yourselves and are not ashamed, and take your garments and trample on them, then you will see the son of the Living One.*

Did he want to open a nudist colony? Well, then, why did the church chastise the cardinals seen naked last year in a gay sauna in Rome?

"Do you have legal problems?" asked Rachid, the colleague who shared Alice's office.

Alice shook her head but leaned nervously over her *Civil Code*. "It's for a client."

"What are you working on now?"

"An old thing that's on its last legs and needs updating."

"Oh, something ancient. I had one of those. Mine was for Duralex, drinking glasses that had been around for at least forty years with no changes. It's the worst kind of client you can have. I much prefer getting hold of a scandal—it's more exciting. How old is your thing?"

Alice made a face. "About two thousand years old."

"Oh boy. Your old thing must be all moldy!"

Alice forced herself to smile, then continued reading.

*Love your enemies, do good to those who hate you.*

At that moment, Arnaud, the head of the Accounting department, came into the office. Arnaud was the kind of unbearable man who was "always right." With dark hair and blue eyes, he would have been rather handsome if his awful personality hadn't made him seem so ugly.

"You made a stupid mistake in your statement for the IKEA file," he said.

Alice looked up. She and Rachid had worked hard for at least two months on IKEA's food scandal, in particular the sale of six thousand chocolate tarts that contained fecal matter.

"What do you mean?"

"You declared mileage for days when there were no billable hours," he said, sounding scornful.

Silence. Alice and her colleague looked at each other, dumbstruck.

"We declare the mileage on the days we travel," said Rachid.

"Oh, really? You travel on the days you don't see your client? That's not logical."

*That's not logical* was the expression Arnaud always used to make someone feel like an idiot.

Alice did not reply and tried to concentrate on her reading to keep from smacking him.

*Bless those who persecute you.*

"I don't know," said Rachid. "Perhaps we traveled the day before to get to a meeting early the next morning?"

"You don't know, you don't know... So how am *I* supposed to know?"

Alice watched him walk away, grumbling, and read out loud very quietly, "Pray for those who mistreat you."

"What was that?" Rachid asked, and burst out laughing.

"Nothing, it's nothing. There's a quote from Jesus in the text. You wouldn't understand."

"Jesus is one of the five great prophets of Islam, my dear."

Great. That was all she needed. Given the present times, that was surely the best argument to get Jesus back in the saddle.

"Imagine for a minute," Rachid continued, "that you worked in Accounting and that you had to put up with Arnaud all day long. It would be hell to have him as your boss."

"Still, you have to see the team of nitwits he's got. That would drive anyone crazy."

Rachid agreed. "Yeah, 'cause he's also bad at recruiting."

*Jesus was also a bad recruiter*, Alice thought. Out of his twelve apostles, one never understood anything and even ended up renouncing him; the second one betrayed him; and all the others ran away like thieves as soon as things started heating up! Not a single one remained faithful to him. And he wasn't a great leader either. He was always complaining about not being able to pass on his faith to his own apostles.

Alice closed the Bible and pushed it away. She felt totally discouraged. For the first time in her career she felt as though she had taken on an impossible task.

She sighed. Next to her, Rachid was on a phone call. She swiveled her chair around to face the plate-glass window. From within the gray ocean of Parisian rooftops, a bell tower rose up here and there, vestiges of a dying religion. Strangely enough, somewhere within her she felt a certain attachment to these buildings, beyond their architectural interest, even if she did hate setting foot in them. Probably a holdover from belonging to the civilization she was part of.

She took a deep breath.

If she used all her goodwill, took all her courage in both hands, set all her skills to work, could she perhaps manage to accomplish something? After all, she had succeeded in bringing clients back to IKEA's restaurants after the company had given them shitty tarts to eat!

# 5

*Rejoice in the Lord!*
*Rejoice in the Lord!*

Sitting at the back of the Notre-Dame Church in Cluny, Alice could barely stop herself from laughing out loud as she listened to the religious songs. It took all her strength to hold back, so much so that her ribs were aching.

Inspired, the two sanctimonious gossips, Germaine and Cornélie, whose dress sense would have made the Catholics of 1793 Versailles look like riffraff, sang the chorus with great gusto:

*I will greatly rejoice in the Lord,*
*My whole being shall exult in my God.*

*Breathe, keep breathing,* Alice thought, to prevent an outburst. *Take short breaths, because if your lungs fill up with air, they might let out the echoing sound of laughter.*

*Hallelujah, for our Lord God Almighty reigns!*
*Sing the glory of his name!*

Jeremy's depressed expression clashed with the joyful melody of the songs.

*Tell of all his marvelous works.*

Her desire to laugh was good for her, given the unease she felt every time she went into a church. It was a disagreeable feeling of being out of place, along with an internal conflict: to make the sign of the cross and behave like a hypocrite, or not do it and feel judged as impious.

*Come now and behold the works of God,*
*How wonderful he is in his dealings with humankind!*

Her father had wanted Alice baptized at birth, more because of tradition than out of true faith, and despite the great reluctance of her mother, who retained a hatred of religion she had inherited from her own mother. Brought up by nuns who themselves had suffered the abuse of power of a poisonous Mother Superior, her grandmother remembered nothing but the bad times. Alice's contact with religion had come to a halt after the baptism. No catechism, nothing. Naturally, she had grown up an atheist.

*Taste and see the goodness of the Lord.*
*Lord, I am yours.*

An idea suddenly came to Alice, and she took out her *Civil Code* to check it. It took her a little while to find the passage she was looking for, even though she had read the New Testament three times to immerse herself in it—one of her old work habits. It was in the Gospel of Matthew, chapter 6, verse 6. Jesus advised people to pray alone at home and not in places of worship. And moreover, he hardly went to them himself: "But when you pray, go into your room, close the door and pray to your Father, who is unseen. Then your Father, who sees what is done in secret, will reward you." So why did these believers in Jesus go to pray all together in a church? Bizarre.

Jeremy then led the parishioners in the recital of a psalm:

> *Have mercy on me, O God,*
> *according to your unfailing love;*
> *according to your great compassion*
> *blot out my transgressions.*
> *Wash away all my iniquity*
> *and cleanse me from my sin.*
> *For I know my transgressions,*
> *and my sin is always before me.*
> *Against you, you only, have I sinned*
> *and done what is evil in your sight . . .*

He went on to give a sermon on original sin and man's sinful nature, which resulted from it. But Alice was positive: not once in the Bible did Jesus speak of original sin. He didn't even allude to it. Not once. Why this discrepancy?

From the back of the church where she was sitting, she had a full view of the nave and choir. When she looked up, she could see a good number of faces carved into the stone. One of them was famous in Cluny: Pidou Berlu, a figure with three faces beneath a single crown.

The parishioners were a tiny handful of people lost in this enormous space. Behind them stood numerous rows of chairs that were disappointingly empty. To the right was an old, dusty confessional made of dark wood. Just the sight of it made Alice feel uncomfortable, without her knowing why.

Directly behind her, religious leaflets were piled up on a table. One of them had a photo of the pope beneath the golden dome of the Vatican.

Jesus had fled when people wanted to make him the king of the Jews, and later on, he had said to a Roman: "My kingdom is not of this world." The Vatican officially claims to be a state, and the pope its sovereign, with a court, subjects, and riches. Its kingdom *is* truly of this world.

She suddenly remembered that when Jeremy had arrived outside the church, his flock had each greeted him with a "Hello, Father," which had caught her attention. She leafed through her *Civil Code* and quickly found what had surprised her. Jesus had counseled: "And do not call anyone on earth 'father,' for you have one Father, and he is in heaven."

Alice frowned. Curious, this religion that strived to do the opposite of what its messiah had said.

> Lord, our Lord,
> How majestic is your name in all the earth!

The singing began again. Alice continued leafing through her Bible. In the Gospel of Luke, chapter 6, verse 46, Jesus asked his disciples: "Why do you call me, 'Lord, Lord,' and do not do what I say?"

After the Mass, Alice and Jeremy walked through the center of Cluny to the town hall garden that overlooked the ancient abbey. Hundred-year-old cedars stretched up toward the blue sky, their majestic branches leaning down to the earth as if bowing in reverence to passersby. They walked in silence, their feet lightly brushing the grass with a barely audible sound. The air had the lovely scent of springtime, making them eager to breathe in deeply. Yet Alice held back, feeling more and more cornered by the mission she had given herself. The wild laughter she had suppressed was a distant memory. Now that she was thinking about her task again, she was once more overwhelmed by a feeling of impotence. How could she coax modern-day people to go and participate in the kind of gatherings called Masses? It seemed beyond her capabilities. The chants were silly, the sermons left you feeling guilty, and the rest was deadly boring. And all of it, with poor Jeremy's look of depression, against a backdrop of sadness.

A squirrel leaped across a bit of grass in front of them and scampered up a cedar tree.

*Okay. Let's start at the beginning.*

"What is your goal as a priest?"

"Excuse me?"

"What is the point of all that? The Mass, everything you do."

He took a deep breath. "To spread the Good News."

"What Good News?"

"The Gospels."

"And . . . if you had to explain that in plain language?"

Jeremy frowned.

She continued, "What exactly do you want to give people?"

"I want to deliver all the truths that Jesus spoke about and that his disciples reported in writing."

"Good. Okay. And . . . what would be the benefits for people?"

She nearly slipped up by saying "consumer benefits," an occupational hazard he would not have appreciated. It was really much easier with the owner of a business. If he made dishwashers, she could easily research why they were useful: they saved time, saved water, and produced sparkling glasses. But with this, she was in much less tangible territory.

By pushing Jeremy to answer question after question, she managed to come to a conclusion that was completely personal, though she was very careful not to verbalize it: if people could internalize Jesus's message, they would be happier. Difficult to believe, of course, especially after having read the Bible, but all right. Fortunately, she was never responsible for the ultimate satisfaction of the customer. In the end, whether the dishwasher made the glasses cloudy or broke down after three months was not her problem.

"You know," she said after a long moment of reflection, "if you want to attract new people, you would be better off talking less about God during the Mass."

"What?" Jeremy choked out.

"The majority of people nowadays no longer believe in God, so there's no point in trying to shock them from the start."

"Shock them? So what do you want me to talk about? The movie that was on TV the night before?"

Jeremy, who was usually so reserved, had difficulty hiding his horror, and Alice regretted her tactlessness.

She continued, but carefully chose her words. "You could emphasize what in Jesus's message can really bring something to their own lives."

*Well . . . if anything can,* she thought.

"I see. A utilitarian vision of spirituality. With personal applications."

34

She confirmed by nodding her head, an apologetic smile on her face.

They continued walking through the garden in silence. Jeremy seemed to be thinking.

"The problem," he finally said, "is that spirituality is the opposite of such an approach. You only find it when you let go of your personal interest to open yourself up to something that is beyond you, something greater than yourself."

Alice made a face. "I used to go to dance classes. No one, absolutely no one, could do a split right away. In every case, you started from what you could do and slowly made progress."

Jeremy did not reply, and Alice felt she had scored a point.

They took a few more steps and sat down on a patch of grass.

"I wanted to suggest something else to you: what if you stopped talking about sin all the time in your sermons? It makes people feel guilty and want to run out of there as fast as they can."

Jeremy shook his head. "How could I leave that out when that is exactly why Jesus died: to cleanse us of our sins?"

She looked doubtful. "Jesus never said that, though he did predict his death on several occasions. And he also didn't seem as obsessed with sin as you all are. His disciples even described him as someone who enjoyed life, who was rather attracted to food and drink."

"You can't seriously mean a thing like that."

She opened her Bible. "I'll show you. I put Post-its in . . . Here, listen to this. The apostle Matthew said of him: 'The Son of Man came eating and drinking.'"

Jeremy did not reply.

"And," she added, "you've made him out to be an asexual prude, even though he never advised couples to abstain or show self-control. Quite the opposite, he told them: 'Do not withhold yourselves from each other'! He even let the courtesans caress

35

his feet with their hair. He didn't have a problem associating with prostitutes either. Your Jesus was the complete opposite of a hung-up ascetic."

Jeremy remained silent. Perhaps he was sensitive to these arguments? *Go on. Don't throw in the towel.*

"I also wanted to discuss the choice of songs."

He frowned. "You mean the hymns, don't you?"

"Yes."

*Don't upset him.*

"I remember hearing some Gregorian chants when I was little," she continued. "They were beautiful, rousing. Why have you given those up for your ... hymns?"

Jeremy burst out laughing. "You are definitely full of surprises! You go from a mind-blowing desire for modernism to a traditionalist return to the past!"

"They're a little more captivating than what you sing today, aren't they?"

*And besides,* she thought, *they're as mesmerizing as can be for shutting down your cerebral skills. Exactly what's needed.*

"But people don't understand Latin anymore! No one would understand the meaning of the words."

*Which would perhaps be better,* thought Alice, who remembered the words chanted during the Mass a few minutes earlier.

"At least admit that the music you use now is unbelievably lacking in artistic merit. You can't feel anything but boredom when you hear it. You need some music that you can feel in your gut, music that touches you deep in your soul. Like Bach, for example! If you used 'Jesu, Joy of Man's Desiring,' you would immediately feel drawn into another dimension. Whenever I hear it, it's so beautiful that tears come to my eyes."

Jeremy shook his head again. "We mostly use it for weddings."

"Who cares? What counts is that it transports you to another world, makes you believe in another reality. You were just talking about opening yourself up to something greater than yourself. Well, when you listen to that, you have the impression that you are connecting... to the creation of the universe! To the Creator himself! Bach could turn the most materialistic atheists, the most Marxist Communists, into believers!"

"But—"

"In any case, you're not going to raise people to a higher level of consciousness with your silly little songs!"

Jeremy was hurt for a moment, and Alice regretted getting carried away. She had, after all, promised herself she would not upset him.

A silence followed that quickly weighed heavily on her. All around her, the garden was empty. Not even a gust of wind to brighten the atmosphere with the rustling of leaves. The tall cedars with their bowed branches seemed despondent on her behalf.

"Okay for Johann Sebastian Bach," he finally said.

Alice smiled with satisfaction, but she also felt admiration for him: not many people would be able to agree to your point of view a few moments after having been upset by what you said. That was certainly evidence of his great soul.

She looked at him without saying anything. He was sitting sideways to her, and his eyes seemed fixed on the tops of the trees far away on the hilltops. What a shame that a man with such a noble spirit seemed so sad, when he obviously would be unbelievably powerful if only he radiated joy.

And besides, wasn't that the crucial message she had to get across to him? How could he ever draw people to his church to bring them the words meant to enlighten them when he himself was so gloomy? But how could she tell him that without destroying him? How could she coax him into working on himself, developing his own self-confidence, learning to like himself, without offending him?

"Have you ever heard of Toby Collins?"

"No."

"He gives seminars on personal development. It's fantastic. I'd love to take you to one."

*Not surprising he doesn't know who he is,* Alice thought. Why be interested in personal development if you believe your salvation is solely in the hands of God?

"You look lost in thought," she said.

He forced himself to smile. "If I take your advice, I'm wondering if I'm going to lose my soul, just to attract more people into my church."

She kept looking at him but didn't reply. He did seem preoccupied, in fact—a little disoriented, like someone who had lost their point of reference. He was staring at the ruins of the abbey. For a few moments, she felt guilty, reproaching herself for interfering in his mission the way she was when he hadn't asked her to do anything. Then, as she remained attentive to his reactions, she felt that he was gradually gaining in confidence.

"What are you thinking about?" she asked.

"The teachings of Meister Eckhart."

"Who's that?"

"A great Christian mystic of the thirteenth century. A professor at the Sorbonne."

"And what did he say?"

Jeremy slowly took a deep breath. "That perhaps you must first abandon God in order to find him again."

# 6

A JAM-PACKED HALL, AT LEAST EIGHT HUNDRED PEOPLE. POWERFUL projectors bathing the stage in an intensely bright light. Very loud, rousing music, as usual. Sitting among the participants, Alice felt elated.

Toby Collins's entrance onto the stage was met with a flood of applause and enthusiastic roars. This blond giant of a man— he was at least six feet five inches—wearing a stylish suit and no tie, walked with his usual mixture of assurance and ease, his smile revealing unbelievably white teeth. Alice watched him with indulgence, without applauding, as if the friendship she had developed with him freed her from this ritual of acknowledgment, which she left to the anonymous crowd. A quarter of an hour earlier, she had taken Jeremy into the green room, where she had been proud to introduce him to Toby, proud to be friends with the famous Toby Collins, the high priest of personal development.

Toby waved to the audience, then began by telling an anecdote that made them laugh. He expressed himself in near perfect French. The theme of the day was self-esteem, a subject that particularly interested Alice. She glanced anxiously over at Jeremy, sitting beside her. It was only now that she understood the enormous difference between the intimate contemplation of his Masses and this great American-style show she had taken him to. She suddenly feared that he might feel completely out of place. For the moment, he was showing no reaction. At least he didn't seem hostile. Not yet, anyway.

"I need a volunteer," said Collins, "to play a game..." He paused.

At least a hundred hands in the audience immediately went up.

"Of mental arithmetic."

All the hands went down at once, which made everyone in the audience burst out laughing.

"I thought France was the world champion in math! Where are the champions?"

The audience was split between those who were laughing and those who were looking at their feet, afraid of being picked. Collins smiled as he walked across the stage, then spoke to a young woman sitting in the first row.

"I'm sure you're good at math."

She vigorously shook her head no, and everyone laughed.

"Come on! Let's encourage her," he said to the audience, who applauded, relieved.

She stood and came up onto the stage, blushing. A brunette with shoulder-length hair, she wore gray jeans and a blue shirt.

"Hello," he said with a big grin. "What's your name?"

"Juliette."

"Welcome, Juliette."

She gave him a timid smile back.

"I'm going to ask you a few fairly simple questions of mental arithmetic. Relax. You can take all the time you want to answer. All right?"

She agreed.

"But I'm awful at math, I'm warning you."

"That's okay," he said in a kind voice. "We're not grading you—it's just a game, and it's just between us. And besides, there are seven hundred ninety-nine people in this room who now feel enormously grateful to you for coming onstage instead of them."

She laughed, and you could sense she was relaxing a little.

"So, to begin with, how much is twenty-four plus thirteen?"

"Twenty-four plus thirteen? Uh . . . twenty-four plus thirteen?"

"Take your time."

"Well . . . thirty-eight? No . . . thirty-nine?"

"You're not far off. Remember, first you add the ones column, four plus three, which makes . . ."

"Seven."

"Bravo. And then the tens, two plus one . . ."

"Okay, three. So thirty-seven."

"Now another one."

"Oh no!" she pleaded.

But he continued, still giving her his most ravishing smile. "Seventeen plus nineteen."

"Oh no. That's even harder."

As red as a beet, she bit her lips.

"Concentrate, calmly."

"I don't know . . . thirty-four? No, I can't do it. I told you I'm no good at math. There's no point."

"Okay. I'll stop torturing you."

The young woman turned around to leave the stage.

"Juliette, wait."

41

She stopped in her tracks.

"You don't want to end on a failure, do you?"

"With this, frankly, I do! I'd rather leave it there."

Everyone in the audience laughed. Alice as well, even though she felt sorry for her.

"Failures are okay in life, if you learn something from them. Now, what have you learned?"

"That I'm awful at math! That I'll never be nominated for the Fields Medal."

Laughter from the audience again, but Collins shook his head.

"No, you didn't learn that here, because you said it from the start. Sorry, but you can't leave unless you learn something."

She sighed and crossed her arms. She no longer seemed ashamed, just frustrated. Collins waited patiently, looking as relaxed as ever.

"I've learned," she said, "that I should never take part in this kind of demonstration!"

Collins gave her a kind smile. "Would you agree to start over again under hypnosis, just a light trance?"

At first, Juliette seemed surprised. She hesitated for a few seconds, then nodded in agreement. "I can't appear more ridiculous than I already have."

"Failure never makes anyone ridiculous. But I'd like to try something."

"Okay."

"So come and sit down," he said, pointing to one of the two armchairs on the stage.

He sat down next to her.

"How do you feel?"

"I've had better days."

Some laughter from the audience.

"Make yourself comfortable and relax. You are *not* obliged to close your eyes, but perhaps you would like to. You are sitting in an armchair and you're relaxed . . ."

Toby Collins's voice, normally so assertive, gradually became lower, slower and slower, gradually softer, until Alice felt like yawning. Juliette closed her eyes.

"You can feel every part of your body touching the armchair . . . from the top to the bottom . . . You can hear my voice . . . Let yourself go . . . calmly . . . quietly . . . You feel more and more deeply relaxed . . . relaxed . . ."

He pronounced each syllable as if he were going to fall asleep before finishing the word, in a deep voice whose echoes could be felt deep within, as if they resonated to the rhythm of one's own breathing.

"That's good . . . yes . . . like that . . ."

His encouragement visibly helped Juliette let herself go, and Toby continued to lead her into a light trance, formulating statements that were sufficiently vague to correspond to her inner being, whatever that might be, and progressively breaking down her defenses. He perfectly mastered all the techniques of the practice. Even though she was just an observer, Alice could feel herself slipping into another state of consciousness.

"And while you feel more and more deeply relaxed, tell me, how much is twenty-six plus twelve. Take your time, calmly . . ."

Juliette remained silent for a few moments, and everyone could tell she felt serene, relaxed.

"Thirty-eight." Her voice was clear and calm.

"That's very good, Juliette," said Toby in a slow, deep voice. "That's very good. Now tell me how much is thirty-nine plus thirteen?"

A brief silence. "Fifty-two."

"That's good, Juliette, very good. And fifty-three plus eighteen?"

A longer silence, but Juliette's face revealed no negative emotion, no apprehension.

"Seventy-one."

"Bravo, Juliette. Now, take your time, and whenever you're ready, you can come out of the trance."

A few seconds later, Juliette opened her eyes and smiled. The audience applauded.

"Hypnosis is not magic," said Collins. "It's just a modified state of consciousness. A state in which you feel liberated from the constraints of your mental awareness, freed from your doubts and fears, so much so that you have full access to your abilities. And I do mean *your* abilities: your answers to my questions came from you, all from you. Before, you underestimated your abilities, and that lack of self-esteem prevented you from using them."

Juliette agreed.

Toby thanked her for her participation, and she returned to her seat as the audience applauded once more.

He stood up and spoke to the room again. "A lack of self-esteem prevents us from having access to our abilities. When I say abilities, I mean all our intellectual, interpersonal, and physical abilities, all our skills, all the strength we have somewhere within us but that we don't always use. You will be surprised to see that you have many more abilities within you than you think."

He paused for a moment before continuing, as if to allow the information to sink in. A profound silence filled the room, while everyone in the audience realized the waste brought about every day by their own harsh judgment of themselves.

Alice recognized herself in that self-critical attitude and was angry with herself for restricting her talents that way, for cutting herself off from her abilities. Then suddenly she realized she was catching herself in the act!

"The good news," said Collins, "because there is good news in this business, is that inversely, knowledge of our skills develops self-esteem, which in turn allows us to have better access to our abilities, so we can succeed in being prouder of ourselves, et cetera, et cetera. It's a virtuous circle! The real question . . ."

He paused again, no doubt to get their full attention.

"The real question is: how to unleash this virtuous circle starting from our current situation. How can we get the ball rolling?"

Alice glanced over at Jeremy. He seemed interested, which reassured her.

"Well, now, the technique that I am proposing is based on a surprising characteristic of our nervous system, which cannot distinguish between the real and the virtual."

Collins looked around the entire audience.

"You don't believe me? Very well. Close your eyes. Go on, everyone close your eyes. Good. Now open your mouth. Imagine that I'm touching a lemon to your lips . . . and that I suddenly squeeze it so the juice slips onto your tongue!"

Alice immediately felt the saliva rush into her mouth.

"Your body reacted as if it were true, didn't it? You knew very well that there was no lemon. But you played the game. You imagined the lemon, you behaved *as if* you were actually tasting the acidic juice in your mouth. And your nervous system reacted accordingly. The virtual has the same influence on us as the real."

Alice started thinking about all the young people who spent their evenings virtually killing thousands of people in their video games. What impact could that be having on them, on their developing personalities?

"The technique I'm proposing to get the ball rolling for self-confidence is based on this characteristic of our nervous systems. Here's the idea: Rather than struggle to convince yourself that you do have the ability to succeed, behave *as if* you had those skills. Have a kind of daydream, imagine that you know what to do, and visualize yourself doing it. You will be surprised by what happens."

Toby stopped to look at someone sitting in one of the front rows.

"You look doubtful."

The reply couldn't be heard clearly, but Toby repeated it for the room.

"You're wondering how this method can give you skills that you don't have. Okay. Well, the idea is not to give you new abilities but rather to allow you to use all the ones you are not using, even though you have them, because of a lack of self-confidence. Self-esteem and confidence allow you to unleash all your abilities and skills to their utmost. But I'm talking too much: the best thing would be to have you test it. Get comfortable."

He returned to his armchair and sat down as well.

"This is a game that each of you will play by yourself, so everything will be confidential. I'm going to ask you to think about your professional situation, your plans if you have any, and I'd like you to jot down on a piece of paper the salary you hope to receive in three years: the highest amount of income you feel capable of achieving three years from now, as well as how you will go about achieving it. I'll let you think for a moment."

He looked at his watch and fell silent.

Alice and Jeremy looked at each other, and she smiled at him. The exercise was hardly appropriate for his situation, and once again, she felt a little embarrassed.

All the same, Alice decided to do the exercise for herself. She took a deep breath. The maximum salary in three years...Not easy to estimate. She considered her current earnings. Okay, what if she got the Qatar International contract? She'd have either a big bonus or a raise. Assuming it would be a raise—she hadn't had one in two years—they couldn't refuse her a 5 to 10 percent increase, given the size of the contract. Let's say 10 percent. And that would be for the first year. For the next two years? Come on, in the best-case scenario she might win a similar contract every year and be compensated each time with a 5 to 10 percent raise. That would make for a salary that was roughly 30 percent higher than her current one. That would really be the best case, if she was very ambitious.

She jotted it down on her paper and glanced over Jeremy's shoulder. On his notepad, he had written down how much he hoped to raise for charitable works in three years. She found it interesting that he felt he had a role to play in that area.

"Is everyone ready?" Toby Collins asked, standing up.

He took a few steps toward the audience.

"You've all written down the maximum salary you feel capable of achieving three years from now?"

He looked around at them.

"Very good. Well, I have some bad news for you..." The room was silent.

"You'll never earn more than that."

The silence in the room grew heavier.

"That's the limit you have given yourself. And, you know, we never surpass the limits we set ourselves."

Alice swallowed. He was right; she could sense it.

"You are perhaps telling yourself that you have to be realistic, that you didn't choose that ceiling by chance, that it corresponds to a rational analysis of your situation, your qualifications, your experience, your merits. But we Americans have an expression to describe all those justifications. Do you know what it is?"

The audience remained silent. He was the only one smiling.

"Bullshit!"

He smiled even more.

"*Bullshit!* All that is *bullshit*! All that is just your sad little justification for your inaction, your fears, your doubts, or even your guilt at being more successful than your parents or whoever."

Alice dared not look at Jeremy again. She had hoped that Toby would not go in that direction, which was a total disconnect from the concerns and values of her friend.

"So now," said Collins, "I have some good news..."

The entire room hung on his every word.

"We're going to shatter that ceiling! We're going to shatter it into tiny pieces! Listen to me."

This last request was totally superfluous.

"Take the amount you wrote down... and multiply it by three. And *that* will be your salary in three years' time!"

He started to laugh.

"I can see your incredulous faces. I'd need at least two hours with each of you to free you from the straitjacket of your psychological constraints. So we'll take the simplest route. This is what you are going to do: Consider your salary multiplied by three and act *as if* it were true. Pretend to yourself that you will actually earn that amount. Project yourself into the future, visualize yourself in three years, as if you were there now, and imagine yourself earning that salary. Feel what that's like, savor the situation, then look at the virtual three years that have gone by and the path you took: what did you do, what actions did you take to get there?"

Alice found it amusing to picture herself enjoying such a high salary, pretending to believe it. Obviously, it was thrilling. She imagined the three years that allowed her to get to that point and immediately pictured a promotion. Of course! She had been promoted to head the Crisis Management department. Besides, didn't she deserve it? Most of the ideas implemented were hers, in the end, even if few people acknowledged it. And she had won quite a number of contracts for the department. She was actually one of their cornerstones.

She continued to imagine herself as a higher-up. What else had allowed her to have that promotion? Perhaps some management training. Yes, of course, to be in the running for that job she had to be credible by acquiring some proficiency.

The longer Alice immersed herself in this fictitious situation, the more she came up with ideas she had not even considered up to that point, and which she might never have dreamed of.

"They'll bring you a microphone," said Collins to a participant who wanted to ask a question.

A young woman made her way into the audience with a cordless mike.

"All that is fine," said the man, "but there's more to life than money. I'm not interested in tripling my salary. What I especially want is to have a sense of fulfillment in what I do."

Several people in the audience applauded. Even though she was a fan of Collins, Alice felt almost relieved at this objection: Jeremy would feel less alone in the room.

Toby gave him a big smile.

"As your great Louis XIV once said: 'I nearly waited!' In general, when I bring up the question of money in France, I immediately have this kind of objection, and here, I found that it was late in coming."

Some laughter from the audience.

"Well, yes. You see, it's completely cultural. In France, people don't want to work for money; they want to work *to be fulfilled*.

In the United States, I have almost the opposite problem: when I talk about professional fulfillment, there is always someone who takes the floor and asks me with an air of total incomprehension: 'What does that mean, "professional fulfillment"? If you succeed, you earn money, and if you earn money, you are fulfilled!' "

More laughter in the room.

"It's cultural. That said, I'm not ignoring your question," he continued, turning toward the questioner. "In fact, I base this game on money because it's very convenient to take a salary and multiply it by three: you can be sure of the quantitative, and it's much easier for everyone to imagine tripling their salary than tripling their fulfillment. But, in fact, if you took part in the game, you probably realized that in the end, we weren't really talking about money. Money is not the essential point of that exercise. It is above all a question of gaining access to our abilities, of freeing the energy that is dormant within us, and money is nothing more than a metaphor for our possibilities, a way of measuring what we give ourselves permission to do, what we allow ourselves to receive."

Alice risked taking another glance at Jeremy's papers. He had written down triple the amount of money he hoped to raise for charity. At least he hadn't been stubborn and had applied the lesson to his own situation.

"Using the virtual in this way to gain access to your real abilities is very effective, and it in no way excludes also developing your self-esteem. Everything is to be gained from loving yourself more."

Toby Collins then launched into a rather complex exercise, with very strict rules, in which the participants, broken into groups of two in the adjacent rooms, were each led in turn to walk a time line drawn on the ground to represent their life's journey. They went backward in time to their childhood to imagine receiving

50

the unconditional love from their parents that they may not have often received and whose impact they might not have felt. They then took the journey in the opposite direction, bringing with them the love they had received virtually to the present day.

When it was her turn, Alice took part in the game and followed the rules step by step, guided by another participant. After this, she felt completely psyched up, and wondered how long that positive feeling would last.

"It's very useful to learn how to love yourself," said Toby Collins to the participants when they were once again all together in the large hall. "I'd even say it is essential. Everything that allows you to make progress on this point is positive, and you have to grab any opportunity to grow your self-esteem."

Alice saw Jeremy make a face that said a lot about his disapproval.

"Now, on this point," said Toby, "a very simple method is to regularly make a written list of your qualities, your skills, your assets: everything that can prove your value to yourself. Don't be content with just doing it once. Do it every week, always write it down, until your self-esteem becomes natural. One of my friends suggests looking in the mirror every morning and saying 'I love you' or blowing yourself a kiss. That may make you smile, but I believe that in this area, any idea is a good one."

Jeremy raised his eyes to the heavens and slowly shook his head.

When they left the hall, it was dusk. They walked in silence, side by side, on the Boulevard de Bonne-Nouvelle to get to the Poissonnière bus stop. Paris was cradled in the soft light of the end of the day, the air lovely and cool. At that hour, there were no more traffic jams and the cars flowed by almost silently.

"Okay... So what did you think of that?" asked Alice.

Jeremy took his time to answer, as if choosing his words carefully.

"Rather interesting."

Hmm...It wasn't a good sign when Jeremy said so little.

"The suggested methods are effective, don't you think?"

"They seem to be."

It was going to be like pulling teeth to get him to say what he really thought.

"But?"

He smiled and said nothing.

"Don't you think it's positive, encouraging, liberating?"

He agreed, but without seeming to fully believe it.

"Don't you believe in the efficacy of his approach?" Alice insisted.

"Yes, I do."

"But?"

"Let's just say...that's not the problem."

"Really?"

He took a deep breath. "In the end, his approach results in reinforcing confidence, pride, self-love...That's very good, but is it really desirable to become an arrogant person full of yourself?"

"I don't think it makes you arrogant. Arrogance and devaluing yourself are two sides of the same coin, because anyone who really has self-esteem doesn't need to prove his worth to others."

"Maybe."

She felt she'd scored a point.

"If I had to use a metaphor," he continued, "I'd say that in the long run, by going to such seminars, you'd become a more beautiful, more balanced, stronger caterpillar. That's very good, but when would you think of becoming a butterfly?"

Alice felt annoyed, without quite understanding what he meant.

"Wanting to become a butterfly before becoming a full-fledged caterpillar—isn't that risking being a malformed butterfly that gets crushed by the first gust of wind?"

"Perhaps... But you see, the point of life is not to reinforce the self. On the contrary, it's when the self is effaced that you can attain another reality."

"That's a little vague for me."

"Letting go of your ego allows you to offer yourself to God and discover true power, the infinite power of God that works through us."

Alice made a superhuman effort not to laugh.

"I know," he said with a kind smile, "that means nothing to you."

She gave in and let herself laugh out loud.

"I'm sorry," she said, still laughing, "but when you talk about offering yourself to God, that gives me more or less the same feeling as if you'd said offering yourself to Santa Claus."

Jeremy sighed and sadly shook his head.

"In any case," she added, "as Desjardins once said, before you can offer yourself up, you have to first belong to yourself."

He seemed to be considering what she'd said, so she quickly added, "Before attaining another reality, you have to know how to live fully in this one."

"To live life fully, the important thing is to be in a place of love, not to stare at your navel. The most important of Jesus's precepts is 'Love each other.'"

Alice looked him straight in the eyes. "How do you think your parishioners can love each other if they don't love themselves? And besides, Jesus also said, 'Love your neighbor as yourself.'"

She felt very proud of having succeeded at quoting Christ. She'd worked hard on her case. In business, nothing was more effective in convincing a client than quoting phrases from the leaders in their own field.

Jeremy did not reply. Silence fell once more as they arrived at the bus stop. Cars passed. One foot off the curb, a pedestrian was trying to cross the wide avenue, but no one was stopping to let him go. On the sidewalk, people walked past each other without even a glance, probably in a hurry to get home.

Jeremy had a faraway look in his eyes.

Now. She owed it to herself to tell him. With a great deal of respect and kindness, she said:

"And how do you think your parishioners can love each other if you ... don't love yourself?"

# 7

"THE CLEANER'S STOLEN SOME DETERGENT AGAIN!"

Alice, annoyed, sat down at the kitchen table. Théo had already started eating breakfast, and his father was buttering his bread. The *cafetière* gave off a smell of freshly brewed coffee that spread throughout the apartment.

"How do you know?" Paul joked. "Did you put a webcam in the bathroom?"

He was sketching a portrait of Théo in a notebook while eating.

"I put a mark on the package. At first, I had my doubts, but now I have proof."

"You put a mark on the package? You're crazy!"

"I don't like being taken advantage of."

"Who cares? A few ounces of detergent won't make any difference."

"That's not the problem! It's a question of trust. I can't

continue employing someone I don't trust. She has the key to the apartment, you know!"

"Just because she took a little bit of your detergent doesn't mean she's going to rob the apartment while you're out."

"That sounds ridiculous to you because you spend all your time with criminals and crooks, but I don't want to let it go. I'm going to fire her."

"You'll be punishing yourself: you're going to struggle to find another one."

"Don't care," she said, buttering some bread.

She stopped to pour coffee into large mugs and switched on the pendant lights above the kitchen counter. When she was in a bad mood, light helped her feel better. The spotlights brightened the yellow paint on the walls, giving the pleasant illusion that sunshine was seeping into the house, even though the sky outside was a dismal gray.

"Want some, Mama?" Théo asked, pointing to a can.

"What is it?"

"It's delicious."

"It's maple syrup," said Paul. "I brought it back from Quebec."

"In a can?"

"That's how they sell it over there. The best kind, anyway. The syrup in the pretty glass jars is for the tourists, and it's not as good."

Alice put a spoonful on some bread, eager to taste it.

"Excellent," she conceded, her mouth full.

"Yes," said Paul. "It's a killer, for sure."

"It's crazy how your job influences your everyday vocabulary."

He smiled. "I visited a sugar shack in Quebec."

"A what?"

"A sugar shack. It's where they boil the sap from the maples to reduce it to syrup."

"Funny name."

"Yes."

"I'm sure they invented the name specially to get the tourists to come."

"And your job makes you see marketing everywhere."

"Papa, will you take me next time?"

"We'll see."

*"Please."*

"Eat up. You're going to be late for school."

Alice had just bitten into her bread when her cell phone rang.

"Hi, Rachid!"

"You want a bit of early morning good news?"

"Go ahead."

"We're short-listed for Qatar International. There are only three firms left. I feel like I can taste the champagne."

"That would be so fabulous!"

"Pauline from the Research department told me. The call went through to her by mistake. You know who I mean?"

"I think so."

"I love her. Very intelligent, brilliant even."

Alice hung up in a bad mood, despite the good news, because of that Pauline, whom she only knew by sight. Why did she feel belittled, put down, when someone else was praised in front of her? She felt it as a kind of wound, as if her own value were diminished.

She took a sip of coffee, and its warmth felt good.

She thought back to Toby's seminars. They helped her feel better and better in her own skin. Ever since the one she'd taken Jeremy to, she had decided to become the head of her department. Once she was promoted, everyone would see her differently, respect her more.

She was so happy to have convinced Jeremy to continue. Not

easy, after that first session two months ago. She'd seen him hesitate, very reluctant at first, then felt a true change in him. His decision had been hard to make, but he was an open person, prepared to hear points of view different from his own, and able to change his mind—a rare quality today.

Once committed, he had made great strides. He'd gone to four seminars, devoured the books she'd lent him, and he'd obviously changed. Toby's system of sponsorship was perfect for her: with one free session for a friend for every five attended in the past, she could educate Jeremy without spending a single penny.

She went to Cluny every other weekend and enjoyed coaching him. Although she had taken on this mission out of friendship and a sense of obligation, to pay her debt to him, she had gradually started to enjoy the situation. She was happy to watch the change happening and felt great pride at her protégé's results: fatalistic and depressed at the beginning, Jeremy had become energized and confident. Never had she observed such rapid progress, as if he had a knack for understanding and applying the concepts of psychology and would soon be able to help others.

He was now beaming during Mass. Resonating with Jeremy's new attitude, Christ's words of love had more impact. And as for the sermons, they were more positive and clearly were felt more by his flock.

He had thus had the courage to make a certain number of changes in church. Alice had observed these from her pew in the last row, which she discreetly slid into once everyone else had taken their seats for Mass. Little by little, she had become familiar with the place and no longer felt oppressed the way she had at first. Her initial discomfort had given way to a more neutral feeling. The church had almost become a workplace like any other to her, a place of business that was simply more serene than the ones she was used to.

She had, it was true, ended up making a deal with Jeremy.

"Can I ask you something?" she had said one day.

"I'm listening."

"I'm happy to help you improve things in church, to touch more people. You just have to make me a promise."

"What?"

"To never talk to me about God."

He had agreed, with a resigned and slightly sad smile on his face.

Alice had learned to observe the little world of the parishioners and enjoyed their inconsistencies, which endeared them to her. How could she not smile, seeing them dressed to the nines to come to Mass, all dolled up to pray to Jesus—Jesus, who had walked barefoot and asked the rich to get rid of their beautiful clothes? How could she not laugh when she heard them gossiping about a neighbor right after they piously listened to a sermon on love and forgiveness?

Alice was quite fond of Victor, the retired winemaker who was half deaf, and his friend Étienne, who stuttered. They made a funny pair.

Several of the parishioners were obviously resistant to the new developments, and the conversations outside the church reflected the dissent in the air. Germaine and Cornélie, the two vicious gossips, were particularly skilled at signaling their opposition through seemingly innocent little remarks.

Her hair dyed as black as a crow, Germaine planted herself right in front of a person, her sharp eyes staring to get their attention.

"He's not bad, Bach," she'd say, "but I enjoyed those little tunes you can hum. Don't you miss that?"

Under her hawk-like gaze, one felt almost forced to agree. Standing at her side, Cornélie, whose yellowish brown hair seemed frozen for eternity under a thick layer of hair spray, nodded, looked inspired, and always supported her accomplice.

"Don't you find that there's something missing recently? Are we about to lose our traditions?"

They scattered little seeds of doubt, and Alice could see that a few of these ended up taking root in some people's minds.

She had also overheard them complaining to Madame de Sirdegault, a baroness whose seat in church—in the first row, near the center aisle—seemed reserved for life, and even remained empty in her absence. She had listened to the arguments of the gossips and promised to have a word with the bishop, which seemed to have delighted them in the extreme, and worried Alice in the same proportion.

Everyone in Cluny knew Madame de Sirdegault, at least by sight or reputation: a woman in her early sixties with a stately demeanor and haughty attitude, elegantly dressed, who always wore a gold cross with a large ruby set in the center. Her husband had left her a few years before, and after the divorce, she had fought to preserve all the privileges of her rank: the large private house, the old Jaguar on its last legs, and especially her married name, which came with the title of baroness—so much more sophisticated than her maiden name, Josette Gross. As soon as she was married, she had taken great care to erase it from every document and every memory. She lived alone after her divorce, alone in that large private house that she no longer had the means to keep up, but she did her best to maintain, with dignity, the position she wished to retain in everyone's eyes.

There was also the nun who slipped little pieces of paper into Alice's hand as soon as she saw her come into the church. They had a few words scrawled on them and were folded over several times. The first time it happened, Alice, surprised, had patiently unfolded the tiny wad of paper as the sister watched her, smiling.

> Blessed are the poor,
> for yours is the kingdom of heaven.

"Why are you giving me this?" Alice had asked.

All the sister did was smile, without replying. Alice kept asking, until one of the parishioners grabbed her by the arm: "It's pointless asking her questions. She's a deaf-mute."

Alice had then made a gesture of thanks without further trying to uncover why the nun had copied down this quote from the Gospels.

The next time, the sister again slipped her a piece of paper, which Alice accepted with good grace.

> Blessed are you when you are hated
> and persecuted,
> and you will be persecuted
> wherever you go.

Alice forced herself to smile, wondering if the sister meant to give her the entire set of Gospels as a flat pack.

The saga had, in fact, continued every time Alice came to church, and she ended up giving the messenger the nickname "Sister IKEA." The poor woman must have been a bit of a simpleton.

In the end, Alice's greatest disappointment was the small number of new parishioners. They had grown from twelve to twenty-one. If she had had to defend this poor result in front of a management committee, she would have loudly and strongly praised the increase of 75 percent, but alone with herself, she felt she had spent a lot of energy with very little to show for it. The newcomers were former members of the flock who had gone astray and finally found their way back to the fold thanks to some positive word of mouth, which of course made Alice feel better about her choices and reinforced her credibility in Jeremy's eyes. But there were still 379 empty seats.

This count would have been enough to discourage the most confident of consultants, but Alice kept in mind the marketing study Nike had once carried out with two students: each was given the task of traveling through Africa to assess the shoe market. The first one had handed in a concise report: "They all walk barefoot. Drop it: there is no market here." The other one had come to a different conclusion: "They all walk barefoot. Get going: there's an enormous market here!"

Alice had not come to the end. She still had one card to play, and she'd been working on it with Jeremy for two weeks. Her ace in the hole had the sweet name of *Confession*.

Confession: the religious act by which the penitent came to admit his sins and obtained absolution seemed totally outdated, anachronistic, and only practiced by those rare, superstitious people who felt the need to reset the marker to zero before taking a plane or giving up the ghost. But Alice saw things very differently. Even though she herself had an almost allergic reaction to the sight of the somber, wooden confessional, the austere booth that looked so harrowing, she had a feeling that confession could bring a good number of people back to church.

With the popularity of reality TV, confession had once again become fashionable, and people loved sharing intimate revelations and admissions of all sorts. It was now common to see movie stars and politicians reveal their weaknesses on television without a trace of shame, confessing to adultery, a penchant for alcohol, or sexual perversions. Any pretext was sufficient to get things off your chest and openly detail your idiosyncrasies. The general public was mad about confessions, and to Alice, that was clearly a marketing tool to exploit. All she had to do was reshape the church act to make it more attractive. While certain of this, she had not yet found the magic recipe.

She simply thought she had to make confession less painful, so the confessor could benefit from advice and thus receive true assistance. In short, to replace the rigid protocol of contrition and absolution with a kind of personalized life coaching.

"It's unthinkable," Jeremy had retorted. "It's been codified since the sixteenth century."

"If you managed to do without it for sixteen centuries, you shouldn't miss it too much if it stops."

He'd shaken his head. "The act of contrition by which the penitent demands forgiveness for his sins is essential," he had said.

"Come on, beating ourselves up is pointless, but finding answers to the difficulties in life that have led us to react badly is constructive. Being aware of my mistakes is a fabulous opportunity to understand myself better and evolve. If I'm content with just beating my chest and having you absolve me, what am I learning?"

She had ended up convincing Jeremy. Now she had to find a way to get the parishioners to come to confession. And the general public as well.

"Do you want some more maple syrup, Mama?"

Alice stared at the tin can.

"What's wrong with you, Mama? Why aren't you answering me?"

She had just had an idea.

63

# 8

"Unbelievable!"

Germaine shook her head. Never had she seen anything like it.

She pulled on her mustard-colored vest so it came down over her long plaid skirt.

"How can you explain it?" added Cornélie in her nasal voice, just as confused.

She turned her head, and her heavily lacquered beige hair followed all in one piece, like a rigid hat.

"I really wonder," said Germaine, sarcastically.

The line in front of the confessional led almost to the door of the church.

Cornélie dipped her finger in the cold water of the font, made the sign of the cross, then dried her hand on her culottes.

"Every day there are more people."

"I told you to ask Father Jeremy."

"I did. He doesn't know," Cornélie said, defending herself.

64

"Hard to believe."

"But he *doesn't* know. He even seemed surprised himself."

"You must not have done it right. I'm just going to have to ask him myself."

Cornélie looked dazed. The slightest reproach seemed to make her doubt herself, which amused Germaine a great deal.

Everyone waited patiently in line. Many new faces, never before seen at church.

Germaine sighed. "It must be because of the times we're living in. People have more and more things to feel guilty about."

Cornélie frowned, looking thoughtful, as if those words had given her food for thought.

"It's been a long time since *we* came to confession," she said after a moment.

"We don't need to."

Cornélie seemed relieved. "You're right. Nothing to do with us."

They could hear the rustling of fabric. Jeremy had just come out of the confessional. He gestured to the penitents to be patient, then quickly headed for the vestry.

"Father..."

"He can't hear," Cornélie whined.

"I'll catch him on his way back."

Germaine followed the priest, who disappeared into the back of the church. She moved silently because of her old sneakers. The door to the vestry was slightly open. Inside was a rather bare, narrow room: a coatrack, a dresser in dark wood with a small mirror on top, and a small tabernacle. The priest must have gone into the bathroom. If she waited, she'd catch him.

A minute later came the soft sound of footsteps. Instinctively, she stepped back into the shadows behind a column and watched. What she saw stupefied and shocked her in the extreme: Father

65

Jeremy, walking past the mirror, had just blown himself a kiss while whispering quickly but distinctly the contemptible words she would never forget:

"I love you."

Horrified, Germaine crushed herself as far back as she could behind the marble pillar until she felt the cold stone of the wall against her back. She held her breath as the priest walked past her, causing the air around her to shift. She shivered in spite of herself, as if the devil himself had brushed against her.

She waited until he had disappeared into the confessional, then crossed the nave again to join her friend, whom she dragged outside to tell her what had happened, bursting with indignation.

The church was bathed in sunlight, and some tourists were admiring the medieval facades of the houses around the square.

"He wasn't like that before," said Cornélie.

"Things haven't been right here for a few months now."

"Yes. Since the beginning of spring. I don't know what's going on."

Germaine nodded in agreement. "I have my own ideas on the matter."

Cornélie opened her eyes wide.

Germaine let the suspense last for a few moments. "Have you noticed that young woman who's been prowling around on Sundays?"

"Brunette, shoulder-length hair?"

"Yes," said Germaine.

"That's Alice, the daughter of the old widower who lives in the house opposite the conservatory."

"I've seen her talking to Father Jeremy several times before Mass, and sometimes again afterward. I'm sure she's got something to do with all these changes."

"But we also talk to Father Jeremy."

"Yes, but with her it's different. I can feel it. I'm sure this is all coming from her."

"Do you think she and he . . . ?"

Germaine raised her eyebrows knowingly.

"But I think she's married."

"In any case, she must be the one who's perverting him. Look at all the bizarre things he has us do in church now. Like giving compliments to our neighbors, pointing out the positive attributes God has given them."

"That's true."

"All that is immoral. We can't talk about our attributes while man is a sinner."

"It's true, man is a sinner."

"And more so woman."

"Indeed!" said Cornélie, seeing a young woman in a low-cut dress walk by. "More so woman."

# 9

THE PATH TO THE BISHOPRIC ENDED IN A NARROW LANE BORDERED by centuries-old thorny thickets. Their dark green needles stood out against a pale blue sky across which raced heavy, dark clouds.

The last time Jeremy had had an interview with Bishop d'Aubignier, a few months earlier, he had admitted his concerns, his doubts about the importance of his mission given the small number of parishioners who attended more out of loyalty than for spiritual reasons. The bishop had played down his qualms: all priests went through a period of discouragement at the beginning of their calling. It was normal, he'd said, sweeping away Jeremy's anguish with a wave of the hand, without truly trying to understand. Jeremy felt like a woman whose depression was ignored simply because "it's normal while you're having your period."

What a change in only a few months. Jeremy now felt confident, serene, at one with his mission, and happy about the results obtained, which he was careful not to take pride in. Alice's methods had indeed allowed him to attract people to the church, especially to confession, where he heard new voices whispering to him every day. Of course, he was no fool—these newcomers were seeking the enlightenment of the priest-coach more than the light of God, but he sincerely believed it was a stepping-stone that could eventually lead to a possible spiritual awakening.

The church was enjoying a true increase in attendance, even if it was far from being full. It was very big, nearly four hundred seats, and Jeremy knew very well that he would never fill it. But now he wisely accepted that fact.

The bishop must be rubbing his hands together in joy. His ambition was no secret—everyone knew he already saw himself as a cardinal. How could he not rejoice in the rebirth of one of the parishes in his diocese? And what a parish! Probably the most symbolic in all of Christianity, yet for two centuries in such a steep decline that it had seemed impossible it would ever recover.

Jeremy gently closed the door of his Renault and looked up at the imposing edifice. Made of white Burgundy limestone with tall, small-paned windows, it had housed authority for centuries.

He walked up the front steps. In the gusting wind, his cassock whipped his legs. He entered and was received by a secretary, who led him in silence down the long hallway to the ante-chamber of the bishop's study, a narrow room with high ceilings and whitewashed walls, and furnished with austere Louis XIII armchairs in dark wood and olive-green velvet.

Jeremy waited motionless for a long moment, then went over to the window. Clouds were gathering outside, passing through the sky and casting moving shadows on the tree-covered hills.

Inside, total silence. If Jeremy hadn't been brought there by a secretary, he would have thought he was entirely alone in a building abandoned by its occupants, with only the wind as company—the wind that was gradually growing louder and stronger. He had waited for so long that he began to wonder whether his host was actually there or had been held up somewhere.

Weary, he finally sat down in one of the armchairs, and at that very moment, the large door to the study opened and the bishop appeared.

Jeremy instinctively leaped up, as if guilty for having allowed himself to rest. "Your Grace..."

The bishop looked him up and down with an enigmatic smile. He was wearing a very silky violet cassock that emphasized his superiority and the authority of his position. Jeremy followed him into his study.

The bishop was a man in his fifties. He had gray hair, intelligent eyes, and a serious face, though Jeremy had seen him be charming to people when he wanted to convince them of something.

The room was enormous, with parquet flooring and a Persian rug. It was bathed in a light that gave new life to the authentic Aubusson tapestries that decorated the walls.

Jeremy sat down in a cane chair beside a long rectangular table while his host picked up some papers from his desk.

"And what news have you from the parish?"

"Very good news," said Jeremy enthusiastically. "I've taken steps to attract new members of the flock, and the results are very encouraging."

The bishop let him speak and went to sit down in the enormous armchair at the end of the table. He was holding documents that he kept looking at as he listened to his visitor. The episcopal ring he wore on the fourth finger of his right hand had a large amethyst surrounded by diamonds that reflected the light every now and then.

"I brought you here," he said suddenly, weighing each syllable, "because I want to have a clear idea of what has been going on in Cluny these past few months."

Silence filled the room. Jeremy swallowed.

Sitting high in his great armchair, the bishop stared at him, a slight smile barely masking the harshness of his expression. The dim light filtering through the clouds made him look pale.

"Is there anything you wish to tell me, Father Jeremy?"

Caught off guard, Jeremy tried to remain calm. "I've implemented some ideas to attract parishioners to church, and—"

"Ideas? What kind of ideas?"

"Let's say that I have tried to . . . modernize some of our practices a little, in order to be heard by a larger number of believers, Your Grace."

The bishop nodded pensively. "And you might not have gone . . . a bit too far, by chance?"

Jeremy looked at him. What had he been told? What was the bishop reproaching him for?

"I act at every moment within my mind and soul to respect the spirit of the Gospels to the letter."

The bishop looked over one of the papers he was holding. "The spirit of the Gospels," he repeated slowly. "The spirit of the Gospels . . . And do you respect equally the spirit of the church you belong to?"

He had spoken those words in a tone of voice that was intended to sound mild, before looking Jeremy directly in the eyes, clearly watching for the slightest reaction on his part.

"I hope so, Your Grace."

"You hope so, or you're sure?"

Jeremy hesitated for a few seconds. "I hope so, most sincerely."

The bishop made a face, staring at him in silence for a long moment. Jeremy felt he was in the hot seat, naked, being evaluated and judged.

The bishop finally sighed slowly and did not press further. To Jeremy's great relief, he moved on to matters of daily life in the parish. Ten minutes later, he stood up to accompany his visitor to the door.

Jeremy followed him, and as he walked around the table, he anxiously looked at the piece of paper the bishop had just put down.

It was a little poster on a pale purple background. The heading read FREE! to attract people's attention. Then followed a few words inviting people to come and talk about personal problems in all confidentiality.

Jeremy froze when he saw the address given, the address of his church. When he saw the rest, he felt a mixture of shame and anger rise within him.

A charcoal sketch of his confessional box took up half the page. Just above it were a few words in a large, playful font:

# The Advice Shack

# 10

A PILE OF GARBAGE.

Enormous.

At the foot of the Montparnasse Tower, just next to the entrance. Overflowing garbage cans, buried under a mountain of black bags, hundreds of them piled up. A disgusting, foul smell. The employees went into their offices, covering their mouths and noses with a handkerchief or a bit of cloth or simply their bare hands. The garbage strike had been going on for only five days and the situation already seemed unbearable. The amount of waste produced by the five thousand employees in the building was quite simply staggering.

A few yards away, the window washer was stepping onto his platform, ready to rise to the top of the vertical face of the office building to do his daily task. The tall Senegalese man was a familiar figure to all the occupants of the building. He enjoyed a kind of permanent right of intrusion at the moment when you expected it least: while you were on the phone, concentrating on a case file while scratching your head, or surfing the internet during work hours. He would appear without warning outside the window, sometimes giving you a knowing wink, sometimes a bright smile, sometimes the opposite: putting on an outraged expression, his eyes wide, pretending to have caught you in some unspeakable act.

Alice had exchanged a few words with him at the end of one workday as he was getting off his platform. She had asked him his secret, as he always seemed to be in a good mood even though his job was hardly an easy one.

"Your job is rather thankless," she'd said, to justify her question.

"Not at all!" he'd protested. "Thanks to me, people can see the world better."

*Thanks to him, people can see the world better*... Alice had walked away, pensive. And what about her? What exactly did she bring to the world?

That morning, standing right in between the garbage cans, the window washer was clearly in high spirits, in the middle of a discussion with an elderly man. Alice walked over to them, breathing through her thin cotton scarf.

"All this chaos seems to make you happy."

"Ha, ha, ha! This gentleman just told me that with all this garbage, the neighborhood is going back to its origins. What a laugh! A chic neighborhood that owes its name to a garbage dump. That's really a good one!"

"But no," said Alice. "Its name is a reference to Mount Parnassus, a sacred mountain in ancient Greece."

"Exactly," said the elderly man, his eyes lighting up. "In the seventeenth century, the students used to come here and recite poems on a mound built of rubble and waste. There was so much that it formed a little mountain, and one sarcastic student mockingly baptized it 'Mount Parnassus.' The term stuck, and the name was given first to the neighborhood, then to the tower."

Alice's cell phone rang.

"Yes, Rachid."

"Hi, where are you?"

"Standing next to a pile of garbage. Where are you?"

"Upstairs, as usual."

"Okay."

"So are you sitting down?"

"Better not to here."

"I've got some unbelievable news."

"Go for it. I'm holding on to the garbage cans."

"We won the Qatar International contract."

The Qatar International contract.

Alice stood there, speechless. She let go of her scarf. Beside her, the Senegalese man had continued his joyful discussion with the retired man. The employees were rushing to get inside the building, holding their noses. She suddenly felt affection for this little group of people.

The Qatar International contract.

They had won it.

Her raise was a certainty, the family trip to Australia, maybe even the promotion...

"They put in a clause with an early deadline," said Rachid. "Can you make an initial brainstorming meeting at ten?"

"Of course. Get the team together. I'm coming up."


An hour later, everyone was gathered around the director of the department, who was the acting head of the project until a permanent one was appointed.

"Let me remind you of the goal," he said. "To restore Qatar's image among the general public in the principal European cities. Let's start with France. Any ideas?"

Alice launched in. If she was hoping for a promotion, she had to be in the spotlight.

"Let's get them to buy a company that's in trouble, a company with some emotional connection, like a traditional business that makes toys in the Jura region that's on the verge of bankruptcy. Then we launch an all-out publicity campaign in the media, like an interview on TV with a worker who thanks them for saving her job. Put yourself in the place of Mr. Average: if the Qataris save the manufacturer of their childhood toys, it's difficult to then imagine them financing ISIS and their executioners, right?"

The director showed no reaction, but she sensed she had hit home. Other people also had ideas, and she did her best to rephrase them in a better way, pacing how often she spoke, positioning herself, apparently ingenuously, as a leader, without overdoing it. After half an hour, the Qataris had a good chance of becoming saints. Suddenly, through the window, Alice saw the cable of the window washer's platform moving, and she thought back to the introspection he had caused in her and the question that had remained unanswered: what exactly did she bring to the world?

She remembered the words Jeremy had recently spoken to her. There are three dimensions to a person, he'd said: the internal, the horizontal, and the vertical. One's inner life, introspection, self-knowledge, were all understandable. The horizontal dimension as well, having to do with one's relationships in life, a sense of brotherhood. But what exactly did he mean by the vertical? That seemed a little vague, not very rational.

She stopped herself from laughing when she saw the Senegalese man's hand emerge from below, then wave about as if he were desperately looking for something to hold on to as he climbed

76

the tower. Finally, all of him appeared. He recognized her in the middle of the group and winked. He was beaming, as usual, despite a salary that was probably minimum wage.

She too was happy when she helped Jeremy, even though she wasn't being paid for it. And was without a title or any official responsibilities.

Very strange.

*     *     *

"How dare you do such a thing!"

Alice started and looked up from the novel she'd been absorbed in. She was sitting comfortably in the old green velvet armchair in the living room, near the window. When she was at her father's house in Cluny, she was used to getting surprise visits. Much less formal than in Paris, relationships here were more natural, and friends often dropped by without being asked.

Jeremy's blue eyes, whose softness normally contrasted with the stiffness of his black cassock and white collar, were now burning with anger.

He was waving the little poster in the air, holding it out in her direction.

Alice gave him her sweetest smile. "Is there a problem?"

"It's completely ridiculous!"

"If it were ridiculous, it wouldn't have been so successful."

"You cannot do something like this without speaking to me about it first!"

"But you never would have agreed."

"And I would have been right to refuse!"

Alice looked at the poster. "Admit that the drawing is good."

"That is not the problem."

Jeremy sighed.

"I'm being blamed for this," he added. "Even the bishop was alarmed and summoned me to see him."

Shit, the bishop. The leadership was getting involved. She hadn't anticipated that.

She looked away, her eyes focusing on the window. The ivory paint was flaking off, dried out by the sun, the same sun that made the grapes of Burgundy produce the best wines in the world.

"I'm really sorry," she finally conceded, staring at the window.

"Not as sorry as I am."

"I realize now that I shouldn't have."

"That's for sure."

"Forgive me."

He didn't reply.

She turned to him. "Please."

She looked at him for a long time in silence, then gave him a charming smile. "Am I *really* going to have to get inside your shack to get you to forgive me?"

Jeremy's severe expression remained for a few moments, then his armor cracked. He suppressed a smile and sadly shook his head.

# Part II

Jesus says: "Let him who seeks cease
not to seek until he finds:
when he finds he will be astonished;
and when he is astonished he will wonder,
and will reign over the universe."

—Gospel of Thomas, saying 2

# 11

THE ANNUAL GENERAL MEETING WAS GOING TO BE ROUGH.

When Alice went into the large conference hall with its tiered seating, she could immediately feel the tense atmosphere. The five hundred employees of the firm sat in near total silence. The convivial mood of former meetings seemed far away.

Alice herself had not been able to calm down for two weeks. The announcement of a general increase in salaries of 0.1 percent, and excluding any individual increases, stuck in her throat.

One-tenth of 1 percent. Worse than nothing: a sarcastic consolation prize that was more humiliating than the outright refusal of any increase. The same egotism, but with less courage.

Adieu, Australia. Goodbye to the family trip she wanted so much.

But what she felt went far beyond dissatisfaction. The worst part was the ingratitude, a kind of scorn, a refusal to take into account the enormous amount of work she had done to win the Qatar International contract, the biggest the company had signed in nearly ten years. Her considerable personal investment had been met with silence, as if it didn't count. She felt unacknowledged, her efforts disregarded, her results ignored. In short, she felt demoralized. Given the general atmosphere, she wasn't alone.

One-tenth of 1 percent.

Obviously, given the circumstances, the revelations by the press were bad—very bad—for the CEO. Served him damned right. How stupid do you have to be, how incredibly stupid, to award yourself a bonus of two million euros two weeks after announcing the annual general meeting and think that people wouldn't know? Obviously that kind of thing would get out! There's always someone, in the Payroll department or elsewhere, who'll leak the information.

Or if it wasn't plain stupidity, it must've been such a sense of superiority that the CEO thought he was untouchable. Maybe the media getting hold of it knocked him down a little? Questioned by a journalist, the board of directors thought it appropriate to respond, in a brief statement, that he deserved the bonus.

Alice noticed the company's union rep a few rows in front of her to the right. He looked in a better mood than the other employees. This situation was a godsend to him. You could tell he felt he was in a position of strength.

The curtain opened and a man came onto the stage, all smiles, whom she recognized at once. It was Sam Boyer, a popular comedian who hosted a weekly TV show. The company had, as every year, engaged the services of a celebrity to be master of ceremonies.

Sam immediately began by telling a funny story . . . that had no effect whatsoever. The audience remained silent. Nevertheless, he didn't get discouraged and continued with a little speech that included references to the everyday life of the company. He had obviously been prepped and had worked on his performance like a pro. But his little witticisms made no one laugh. Their hearts weren't in it, clearly. Sam continued, unshakable, and Alice felt a certain respect for him. Not easy to do a comic routine in front of five hundred people who want to do anything but laugh.

Sam then introduced the finance director, who came onstage looking like a depressive who'd run out of antianxiety medicine one rainy Sunday night in November.

With half a dozen bar charts, three pie charts, four flow charts, and a bunch of scattered figures, he laboriously tried to show that the results were both very good and very precarious. But the flagrant imperfections of the formatting of the slides fooled no one: everything had been reworked in haste at the last minute.

Next came the marketing director, much more at ease, smiling, as if to show that he had nothing to feel guilty about. He was happy to reply with humor to the jibes Sam Boyer made at him. Alice felt the atmosphere relax a little.

Then it was the CEO's turn.

He crossed the stage in a dead silence. He didn't smile, but he didn't look uncomfortable, as his finance director had. He'd clearly worked on his attitude: confident without being arrogant.

Sam Boyer left the stage. Personal choice? Request by the staff?

The boss began his speech, leaving out the few emotional effusions he'd pretended to feel in previous years toward "the best team in the world." He stuck to the facts, rapidly sweeping aside the past year to talk about the future, the only possible area where he could hope to reinvigorate his troops by making them dream of the promising prospects before them.

He was met with icy silence, but since he had been expecting it, he continued to run through ideas without seeming to be concerned in the least. In previous years, at the end of his speech, he had allowed time for a Q&A with the employees. Would he risk doing that this year?

The audience seemed to be paying close attention to his words, much more than usual, as if everyone were lying in wait for the moment when he would tackle the thorny question of the cap on salaries.

But he was coming to the end of his speech without having raised the matter, and suddenly Sam Boyer leaped onto the stage like a devil jumping out of a box.

"Is this going to last much longer?" he said in a tone of voice that was meant to sound insolent.

The CEO pretended to be surprised.

"We've had enough!" said Sam. "We want to get to the buffet! All these speeches are well and good, but *we* came to eat! Come on, everyone! Let's go! And may the fastest among you stuff your faces!"

The CEO pretended to laugh heartily while folding his papers to follow Sam in the direction of the buffet.

"Not so fast!" a voice trumpeted.

Everyone turned to look at a man who had stood up in the middle of the audience. The union rep.

Beneath the lights, the CEO hesitated for a moment, then stopped at the edge of the stage.

"A question," said the rep.

The CEO, stoic, decided to listen to him.

"With inflation at 0.3 percent and the increase in salaries announced as 0.1 percent, that means a decrease of 0.2 percent in salary. How can you justify the drop in purchasing power given the current positive position of our company?"

The tension in the silent room was palpable. Electric.

"I understand your frustrations," said the CEO, looking

empathetic, the way his advisors had obviously coached him to do. "But it is my duty to ensure continued good results to prepare for the future and thus guarantee that you can all keep your jobs."

The following question, which everyone expected, sounded like the cracking of a whip.

"In that case, doesn't your bonus of two million euros put that goal at risk?"

The eyes of the five hundred employees were riveted on their boss. Alice watched the scene, detached.

Her lack of motivation made her indifferent. She didn't feel it had anything to do with her anymore.

"It was a decision by the board of directors, and they have the final word."

Alice sighed. The reply had been just as boring as the question. The situation was sufficiently eloquent in itself. There was no need for a debate, or even comments.

Alice started thinking of Jeremy, the advice she'd given him, the changes he'd made, the success he'd had. Of course, she hadn't won her bet—they were far from having one hundred people come to Mass on Sundays. But a lot of people went to confession. Most important, she felt that Jeremy was much happier at his job, which had been her main goal. She had loved using her energy and creativity to serve a cause that was so strange to her. She was an atheist, practically drenched in antireligious culture since childhood. She thought of Jesus again, thought of his disarming words, which had succeeded in having an impact on his followers during his lifetime.

"And what if he was an imposter?" she had asked Jeremy. "It seems that many people at the time tried to claim they were the Messiah the Jews were waiting for."

Rather than being offended, Jeremy had laughed. "The

Messiah they expected was supposed to be a warrior. It was a harsh time, when strength was valued. And then along comes Jesus, who tells people, 'Love each other.' Those words may seem banal to you today, but when you put yourself back in the context of those times, it was totally absurd. Revolutionary. That wasn't at all what they wanted to hear. By speaking that way, he was much more likely to be rejected than to please people."

If he wasn't an imposter, Alice thought, then he was probably a kind of sage, a charismatic great thinker. But could you be a sage and still formulate precepts as astonishing as "If someone slaps you on the right cheek, turn to them the other cheek also"?

In the auditorium, tension was rising all around Alice. The union rep was getting annoyed, and the voices were getting louder. She could sense a wave of resentment aimed at the stage.

*Turn the other cheek*...How was Jesus able to attract scores of followers by saying such things?

A few insults were hurled at the CEO. The employees' contained anger was beginning to be awakened. It was going to spin out of control.

Suddenly, Alice felt something strange within her. Like an idea that came not from her mind but from her gut, from deep inside her. Something within her pushed her to act according to this absurd Christian precept. And the more she saw everything getting out of control, saw the clash of so much negative energy, the more she felt she simply had to act.

So despite the stage fright she felt every time she tried to speak in public, she stood up and waved her arms in the air to get people's attention.

"Excuse me!"

They finally noticed her, and strangely, when she began speaking to the CEO, everyone fell silent.

"We read in the press that you stated you deserved your bonus. Since you said it, it must be true."

Alice saw hundreds of people turn toward her in disapproval.

"Since your bonus was deserved, it's fair that we lower our income so you can have it."

A hum of disgusted protests rushed through the room. Alice felt the weight of reproach, incomprehension, and betrayal fall on her. She glanced over at the union rep, who was giving her a hateful look.

On the stage, the CEO stood dead still, not understanding what was happening.

She continued amid the harrowing silence. "I therefore officially request that you lower my salary so you can increase yours."

General astonishment.

Alice walked down the center aisle toward the stage. Everyone looked at her with hostility and repugnance. A wave of whispers accompanied her as she walked.

"You deserve it!" she shouted at her boss, finding it within herself to sound sincere.

He took a step as if to leave.

"Wait!"

He seemed to hesitate for a moment. She took advantage of it.

"Don't run away!"

Now he couldn't leave without looking like a coward.

He stopped in his tracks and faced her as she approached. She hoisted herself onto the stage.

Blinded by the lights, she took a few steps toward him, then opened her handbag and searched through all the junk it contained. Paul always made fun of her when he saw her looking for something in her purse.

Now, in terrifying silence, here were five hundred people watching her. She could feel their judgment, their scorn.

Those damned lights lit her up but didn't light up the bottom of her bag.

She finally got out her wallet and quickly opened it. She found a fifty-euro note and offered it to her CEO.

"Please accept my contribution to compensate you for what you deserve."

Visibly shocked, he stepped back, dumbstruck, almost frozen to the spot.

Alice then turned to the audience and shouted: "I invite everyone to do the same! Come on!"

There was a lull, a tense silence, as if people needed some time to get over their astonishment and realize what was going on. Then she felt something shift in the air. The tide was turning.

A few seconds later, the stage was rushed by employees waving banknotes or checks under the nose of the CEO, who stood scarlet with shame. Very quickly, the stage was full. A crowd of people surrounded the CEO, who was stunned by the shouting and dripping with sweat because of the heat of all the bodies and the lights, unable to escape this surge of intense generosity.

It took the security guards more than an hour to extricate the boss and clear the room.

The next day, a memo from the board of directors stated that the CEO was relinquishing his bonus and that there would be a general salary increase of 5 percent.

# 12

ALICE WAS NOW CONSIDERED A HERO IN THE OFFICE. THERE were endless messages of sympathy, compliments, invitations, and thanks to her via email, text, or just verbally as she walked down the hall.

Some people tried to explain what she had done, perhaps to dissociate themselves from it and regain their obligatory neutrality. It was commented on with reference to philosophers she hadn't read or psychological movements and schools of thought that were in fashion.

"Very Taoist, what you did yesterday!" said one of her colleagues from the Public Relations department of the ready-to-wear section.

"Yes," confirmed someone else from the Perfume department. "Very interesting that you embodied the spirit of Taoism that way."

That evening, Alice thought about all those strange references.

No one, absolutely no one, had seen her act as inspired by Christianity.

Of course, it was much more trendy to allude to Taoism than to Christianity. Jesus was most likely a has-been. And to Alice's professional entourage, the optics of something was essential. Nevertheless, those erroneous attributions intrigued her, gave her a desire to dig deeper into the matter.

She went into a bookstore and was advised to start with the Tao Te Ching of Lao Tzu, the fundamental work on Taoism. She went home, let the nanny leave, and had a quick dinner with Théo before putting him to bed. Paul would probably be home late, as usual.

She stretched out on the sofa, a cup of steaming-hot citrus green tea on the coffee table, and picked up the mysterious work.

A preface by the publisher introduced Lao Tzu: An archivist in the court of the Zhou in China in the sixth century BC, he decided one day to leave the empire so as not to passively watch its decline. Just as he was about to cross the Great Wall of China, an officer who guarded the western gate convinced him to write down a summary of his wisdom. And that is how the Tao Te Ching was born.

She started reading the work. It was a collection of numbered precepts. There were eighty-one in all, and each one seemed to fit on a single page. It would be a quick read. And yet, right from the first lines, she felt she should have made herself a whiskey and Coke: more anachronistic than green tea, of course, but much more effective for relaxing and preventing a headache.

# I

*A path that can be traced is not the eternal path:*
*the Tao. A word that can be spoken is not the eternal word.*

*Without a name, it is the source of heaven and earth. With*
*a name, it is the mother of ten thousand beings.*

*Thus, an eternal non-desire represents its essence, and through*
*eternal desire it manifests its limit.*

*These two states coexist and are inseparable, differing only*
*in name. When thought of together: a mystery! The mystery*
*of mysteries.*

*This is the portal to all essences.*

Fine.

Okay.

What if she put the TV on? A nice little American series, or even a TV reality show so she could fall into a carefree coma?

*Come on. Make a little effort.*

She took a sip of tea.

Another page.

She read the first sentences and was about to stop before falling asleep when one saying caught her attention.

*The holy man produces without owning anything, works*
*without expecting anything, accomplishes his laudable works*
*without becoming attached to them, and for that very reason,*
*those works survive.*

The relationship to her situation amused her. She too had helped Jeremy without expecting anything in return, without taking credit for the results. This book was describing her as a saint! Definitely a good book, then!

Alice kept going, skimming through the precepts that seemed abstract or obscure, sometimes even incomprehensible. Amid a flood of mysterious words, she managed to find several interesting ideas that encouraged her to continue reading.

But after a while, a completely unexpected feeling rose within her. A feeling of déjà vu. The mysterious words she was leafing through reminded her of other words that were just as mysterious, words she had done her best to read and reread without managing to completely understand them, words that were sometimes so strange that she had made fun of them. The words of Jesus.

How was it even possible? Six centuries separated the two men, six centuries and thousands of miles, during eras when people rarely traveled, and well before the invention of printing.

Troubled by her discovery, she rushed to find her Bible–*Civil Code* and started reading the Tao Te Ching again from the beginning to track down the similarities.

As she discovered them, she wrote them down, and little by little, her surprise was transformed into enthusiasm as she measured the extent of her discovery.

Sometimes Jesus's words seemed to echo those of Lao Tzu, as if he were answering him:

**Lao Tzu:** *My heart is the heart of someone simple of spirit.*
**Jesus:** *Happy are the poor in spirit.*

At other times, their words were entirely alike:

**Lao Tzu:** *When the holy man has given away everything, he possesses even more.*
**Jesus:** *Give, and ye shall receive a hundredfold.*

Even the most incomprehensible, the most unacceptable, words were very close in meaning:

**Lao Tzu:** *Take upon yourself the stains of the kingdom . . . and you will become the king of the world.*
**Jesus:** *Blessed are you when people insult you, persecute you.*

Sometimes the vocabulary was different, but the ideas were virtually the same:

**Lao Tzu:** *The holy man has no desire other than to have no desires.*
**Jesus:** *Watch and pray so that you will not fall into temptation.*

And there was the same call to humility:

**Lao Tzu:** *He who puts himself into the light remains obscured. He who is satisfied with himself is not valued.*
**Jesus:** *If I glorify myself, my glory means nothing.*

**Lao Tzu:** *By putting himself last, the holy man shall be first . . . He who is strong and great is in an inferior position.*
**Jesus:** *For those who exalt themselves will be humbled.*

Both men lamented the difficulty of putting their ideas into action:

**Lao Tzu:** *My precepts are very easy to understand, very easy to follow, yet no one can understand or follow them.*

**Jesus:** *Why do you call me, "Lord, Lord," and do not do what I say?*

Both of them warned against the dangers of obsession with material goods:

**Lao Tzu:** *There is no worse disaster than the desire to possess.*
**Jesus:** *It is hard for someone who is rich to enter the kingdom of heaven.*

And sometimes with very similar metaphors, very similar words:

**Lao Tzu:** *A room full of gold and jewels cannot be guarded. Taking pride in having many riches and glory will draw misfortune upon you. When a good work has been accomplished and becomes celebrated, you must step back into the shadows: this is the path to heaven.*
**Jesus:** *Do not store up for yourselves treasures on earth, where moths and vermin destroy, and where thieves break in and steal. But store up for yourselves treasures in heaven, where moths and vermin do not destroy, and where thieves do not break in and steal. For where your treasure is, there your heart will be also.*

The same invitation to rediscover the essence of a child:

**Lao Tzu:** *Whoever holds the greatness of virtue within him is like a newborn child: poisonous beasts do not sting him, wild animals do not tear him apart, birds of prey do not carry him away.*
**Jesus:** *Whoever takes the lowly position of this child is the greatest in the kingdom of heaven.*

They even seemed to share the same view of death:

**Lao Tzu:** *He who dies without ceasing to be has attained immortality.*

**Jesus:** *Unless a kernel of wheat falls to the ground and dies, it remains only a single seed. But if it dies, it produces many seeds. Anyone who loves their life will lose it, while anyone who hates their life in this world will keep it for eternal life.*

That night, Alice went to bed feeling very intrigued.

Either Jesus had copied Lao Tzu or their words, so unclear to her, contained such fundamental truths that they were universal.

And if that was the case, she was determined to decipher them.

# 13

"F<small>ATHER</small>!"

Alice's voice echoed beneath the high vaults of the nave.

The man turned toward Alice. He had white hair and many wrinkles on his face. The light filtering through the windows dimly illuminated his deep-set hazel eyes. He looked at her closely for a moment, with kindness.

"My child..."

"I'd like to ask you a few questions...about the Bible."

He looked at her and smiled. "I don't think I know you, my child. Are you new to the parish?"

"No, I'm...I'm just passing through Paris. Well...I mean... passing through this neighborhood and...I had some questions I thought of. Do you have a moment?"

She saw him smile at her awkward explanation and realized he wasn't the kind of man to judge.

"I'm listening."

She thought back to the questions she had prepared. This time she didn't want to screw up. She needed clear answers. The day before, the priest from the church near her place, a chubby, jovial man, had given such vague answers that she had wondered whether he was making fun of her.

"Okay, my questions are about the words of Jesus, words that are very well known. But I realized that I actually barely understand what they mean."

"Ask me."

"They concern the statements he makes, you know: 'Happy are the poor in spirit,' 'Happy are the afflicted,' et cetera."

"The beatitudes."

"Right. Well, thinking about them, their meaning escapes me a little. For example, take the first one: 'Happy are the poor in spirit.' What *exactly* did he mean by that?" She had carefully articulated "exactly."

"I see what you're getting at... That beatitude has been mocked the most because its translation has been distorted for a long time. I've read and heard endless times 'Happy are the poor *of* spirit' or 'the *simple* of spirit,' and that's probably where the expression the 'happy fool' comes from. The correct translation should be 'poor in spirit,' and that simply means those who are poor in their spirit, in their hearts."

"All right, but how does being poor in spirit make people happy?"

"Each beatitude represents a situation that is not, in fact, considered as blessed in the earthly world, such as poverty, hunger, or humiliation, and Jesus affirms that each one of those things will bring happiness to a person in the kingdom of heaven."

The kingdom of heaven, the kingdom of God—all those expressions annoyed Alice: how could anyone in the twenty-first century believe there was a God somewhere in the sky? In the years since airplanes and missiles had been flying through it and astronomers had been examining it, they surely would have discovered a God somewhere if there was one! *Fine. Let's move on. Just remember that Jesus promised happiness to people who suffered the situations described.*

"And what allows him... to state that?"

He smiled, and his wrinkles stood out even more around his hazel eyes.

"The paths of the Lord are sometimes mysterious, my child."

"Perhaps, but I would really like to understand."

"We can't understand everything, because God is beyond our comprehension. We cannot understand all his thoughts. The words of his son are there to guide us. It's up to us to follow them in hope, in faith."

Alice quickly understood that she wouldn't get any of the explanations she was looking for, no more than the day before. Too bad Jeremy was incommunicado. He was at a retreat for two weeks at the Lérins monastery, according to what his mother had said on the phone. In any case, she would have been a little embarrassed to ask him for explanations of the Bible now, after having finished advising him. Doing things backward was never well regarded.

Her investigations of Taoism had hardly been more fruitful. Taoist monks were not roaming the streets in Paris, and the one she had managed to find—with the greatest of difficulty—spoke French so badly that their dialogue was limited to a few polite, smiling exchanges that were charming but superficial.

She was beginning to believe that her research would lead her nowhere. Either the clergy were jealously guarding the secret of the meaning of the precepts or they didn't understand them themselves. And yet there was *definitely* something to discover in the Christian and Taoist scriptures. She could feel it deep down inside her, and her instincts were rarely wrong.

She hated being caught in a situation with no obvious solution. Nothing was more annoying.

Before going home, she headed to the supermarket at the end of the street to do some quick shopping.

What if the solution was to try to understand by experimenting herself? Wasn't that what she had done by turning the other cheek to the CEO? What we experience in life is more educational than what remains on the intellectual level, isn't it?

She went into the supermarket. *Don't forget the laundry detergent—there's none left.* She felt a flash of annoyance when she thought of her cleaner's continual pilfering.

At the entrance to the store, behind the row of checkouts, Catholic Relief Services had set up a stall with large containers in which clients could leave purchases that would be distributed to the poor. A lot of people were in the aisles. The busiest time of day, after work.

*Okay, let's do an experiment.* But where to start?

With the most difficult thing, of course. Always start with the most difficult to get it over with.

*Blessed are you when people insult you, persecute you.*

One really had to be a masochist to put oneself in a humiliating situation in order to find happiness.

At that moment, she was pushing her cart past the condom shelf. She stopped dead, remembering how embarrassed she'd felt the last time she put a box of them on the checkout girl's conveyor belt.

It was too much of a coincidence. A true Jungian synchronicity. She *had to* seize the opportunity; it was necessary. She knew that very well. Fill her cart with condoms, spread them all out on the checkout girl's conveyor belt, taking her time, then after she had paid for them, take them all to Customer Service and ask for a refund. Great: two opportunities to be humiliated, one after the other!

She felt her hands getting moist just at the thought of it.

It was no time to chicken out. Otherwise she wouldn't learn anything. She looked around her, took a deep breath, exhaled, breathed in again, then began.

A minute later, she was in line at the checkout, her heart pounding. She was as nervous as if she had to speak in public in front of an audience of two thousand. Lots of people around her. The cashiers were busy: scanners were beeping all over the place, credit cards snapped, bills flew about.

In front of Alice was a granny, and in front of her, a teenager who was putting packs of Coke on the conveyor belt. Just behind her, a man in his early forties, handsome, with brown hair and blue eyes. *Help!*

It was the granny's turn in front of her. She put down two yogurts and a package of crackers. Alice bit her lip, a lump in her throat.

The cashier took the yogurts, and the conveyor belt moved, leaving room for the next items.

Alice could feel her heart beating faster and faster. She wanted to run away.

*Carry it through to the end. Experiment.*

*Now.*

She took a deep breath and put the first package of condoms on the conveyor belt. Then the second. The third. Then she grabbed them four at a time.

The granny was looking for her change.

The condoms piled up, a veritable mountain of them. Alice

100

added the last package and glanced furtively behind her. The handsome man smiled at her.

*Lord.*

The checkout girl was actually a woman, and well into her fifties. She had short hair pushed behind her ears. She took the first package without the slightest reaction. Alice took a breath.

"Are they all the same?" she asked, pointing to the pile.

Alice stammered without thinking, "Yes...yes, yes."

The checkout woman scanned the first package, then let the others go by as she counted them. Thankfully, she handled them with the same neutrality she would herbal tea.

Suddenly she shouted, "No, look, they're not all the same! There are regular ones and then some are extra large. That's all wrong! Look, there are even some extra extra large."

Alice nearly choked. "Umm...yes," she admitted, forcing herself to laugh to seem relaxed.

"You've made a mistake. Do you want to exchange them?"

"No, no...I'll keep everything," she rushed to answer, before regretting it when she realized what that implied.

The checkout woman swept all the packages back so she could scan them one at a time. Several fell on the floor. Alice bent down to pick them up. So did the handsome man...who handed her a box with a knowing smile. Alice felt herself turn bright red.

The beeps of the scanner echoed, each one a sharp little needle of shame, as she watched the boxes go by one by one.

She quickly paid and threw everything higgledy-piggledy into the cart.

"Have a good evening," said the handsome man, looking at her with a twinkle in his eyes.

She fled.

Out of the question to go to Customer Service for a refund. Too bad!

She quickly dumped everything from her cart into one of the Catholic Relief Services' containers.

"Thank you, madam, for your generosity," a very aristocratic woman in her sixties said. Alice nodded and walked away as the woman was putting on her glasses, a box of condoms in her hand.

# 14

A TOTAL FAILURE.

Nothing to be learned from that disastrous experiment.

Humiliated, yes; happy, no. And there had been not a glimpse of the "path."

Once home, Alice paced up and down the living room while the water was boiling for her tea. She was angry but refused to admit defeat. She refused to believe she couldn't learn anything from the mysterious precepts. No one had been able to explain them. Okay. Experimentation hadn't worked. There was no denying it.

Well...she would try a new experiment.

Never abandon anything after a single failure. She had promised that to herself after failing her baccalaureate exam at eighteen. She had passed the following year and made it through the competition to get into the École Libre des Sciences Politiques two years later. Nothing is ever beyond all hope.

And, sure, she had felt humiliated at the supermarket, which wasn't fun for anyone. But after all, she was still alive! So she'd already learned something.

It was 6:15. She still had an hour before the nanny arrived. A new idea had just come to mind, and she wanted to try it out *immediately. Don't finish the day on a failure.*

She ran into her bedroom and took off her high heels, her fitted suit and silk blouse. She emptied her closet and found an old pair of jeans that she'd cut up years before to turn into a pair of long shorts. She put them on and looked at herself in the mirror. They were shapeless, and her bottom looked deformed. Without a hem, several inches of the edges were frayed to right below her knees.

She put on the old sneakers she kept for jogging through puddles on winter evenings. Finally, she slipped on a sleeveless T-shirt her friends had given her for her bachelorette party: white with a large orange and yellow Superman S in the center, and in big, fat orange letters, the words SUPER MAMA.

She ran into the bathroom and rubbed off some of her makeup, let her hair down, took off her watch and jewelry, then glanced in the mirror.

She looked like no one in particular.

*Courage.*

She emptied the contents of her handbag into a plastic shopping bag and ran toward the building's elevator. In the foyer on the ground floor, she ran into the downstairs neighbor. The woman looked at her condescendingly without even bothering to say hello.

Alice put up with the humiliation, which was no worse than the unbelievable irritation she normally experienced when she felt belittled in the presence of this woman, or any other woman she found more sophisticated than herself.

A short walk and five subway stops later, Alice was at her final destination.

Hermès.

The windows of the famous boutique on the Faubourg Saint-Honoré were lavishly decorated with the new spring-summer collection, tastefully arranged, and with price tags that seemed to be aimed at a Japanese or Middle Eastern clientele.

At that very moment, a European woman proved her wrong. She approached the beautiful polished dark wood door, which a doorman was quick to open for her, greeting her respectfully.

For the first time, Alice hesitated. Was she really going to inflict shame on herself by risking the disapproving looks and even comments of the saleswomen? And what if she was escorted out? What if they wouldn't even let her in? What exactly was she hoping to learn from this?

*Idiot! It's exactly because you don't know that you need to do it!*

What if she was doing this for nothing? What if she learned nothing from it, like at the supermarket? And why hadn't she learned anything then?

Because she was fighting her shame, she thought. She had done everything to avoid feeling ashamed, averting her gaze, forcing herself to think about something else. In the end, perhaps she hadn't actually *experienced* her humiliation?

*Good grief, you're turning into a masochist, you poor thing.*

In his tragedy *Agamemnon,* didn't Aeschylus ask us to suffer in order to understand? She had to experience the humiliation, let herself feel it, listen to and understand her sensations.

*Go on.*

She took a deep breath, then walked toward the majestic door.

The doorman did not open it—she had to push it open by herself and go inside. He looked her up and down but said nothing.

The soft lighting and delicately perfumed atmosphere created a very refined ambiance. It was the first time she had gone into this pinnacle of Parisian luxury, and she would have preferred to experience it in other circumstances than the ones she was in now, with a knot in her stomach and a weight on her chest.

*Relax, it's just an experiment.*

She glanced around and saw several saleswomen look her up and down with disdain.

*That's it. I'm ashamed.*

She felt a mixture of shame and anger, anger toward these saleswomen, anger at the doorman, anger at Jesus with his unbelievably stupid precepts.

*I would have liked to see him at Hermès, with his tunic and sandals!*

There were customers here and there—not a dense crowd, but a good number all the same. She turned around and saw a young woman come in. A saleswoman, all smiles, walked straight over to welcome her. No one greeted Alice. She had been well and truly ignored.

Obviously, the way she was dressed demonstrated a lack of means to buy the articles for sale. And strangely, Alice found that humiliating in itself: she felt as if she were wearing a sign around her neck that said NOT RICH ENOUGH TO BUY. And that made her feel like setting everyone straight by shouting, "Actually, I *can* afford these things! This is just a game, an experiment! I have the money to be a customer like anyone else."

But why? Why did she want them to know?

*I want them to know that I am worth something.*

And yet she knew very well that her worth had nothing to do with her income. *We aren't what we earn, that's obvious!* But she must have believed the opposite a little, deep down... and immediately she got annoyed with herself.

*In any case, why should it be important that these strangers see my worth?*

It was true: she didn't know them and would never see them again. She again felt guilty when she realized that her sense of self depended on how others saw her, on their judgment. What was the point of working on personal development for years to still end up here?

*I am not my clothes! I am not my money! I am not what other people think of me!*

She felt the need to shout these truths in her own mind to be convinced once and for all, and to be free of these idiotic illusions, which had been put into her head against her will, illusions that remained, despite the work she had done on herself, illusions that did not even match up to her own values.

And suddenly she realized the negative expressions she had used: *I am not my clothes, my money, et cetera.* The rejection of those illusions did not state who she was. She felt a kind of vertigo: how can you refuse to be what you aren't, if you don't know what you are?

Around her, rich customers walked by without looking at her. The saleswomen continued to haughtily ignore her. To these people, she actually did not exist. She was nothing more than what she was *not* in their eyes.

Unsettled by her thoughts, her pride wounded, she continued to walk through the boutique, under the dimmed lights, on the thick carpet, amid the luxurious clothing and expensive leather goods. And the more she walked, the more detached she felt from her surroundings, from the people there, and even from herself. Her humiliation slowly transformed into a sort of internal void, a soothing nonexistence.

She strolled through the rooms and different floors of the boutique as if she were floating through the air, and from this state of nonexistence, a feeling of freedom gradually emerged, a sweet, light kind of freedom, a vague feeling that emanated from deep within her, totally liberating her from the habitual pressure of appearances. She let herself taste that strange, new sensation, savor it, and suddenly she felt alive, truly alive.

She was no longer that floating cloud she had been a few minutes before. On the contrary, she now felt more and more present in her body, more and more conscious. Conscious of existing, conscious of being herself, and even of existing beyond herself, beyond the limits of her body. This consciousness was mixed with a feeling of extraordinary joy that rose from within her, a joy that grew and grew, radiating through her entire body, her mind, and all around her, like an invisible but very real aura. It was a kind of joy greater than all the moments of bliss she had known before.

There she was, ugly, sloppily dressed, ignored by everyone, and she felt more alive than ever.

# 15

CLUNY IN NO WAY RESEMBLES THE TYPICAL VILLAGES THAT HAVE been renovated down to the smallest detail and that, at first glance, are so appealing until you start wondering if you haven't somehow landed in Disneyland. Cluny is quite the opposite: it is an authentic medieval city whose beauty is not obvious at first. The narrow streets leading to the town center can give visitors who come for a short visit the impression it is somewhat worn, sad, and with nothing of interest apart from the monuments that tourists find attractive. Cluny's true beauty appears to people who allow themselves the time to get a feel for the place, to look beyond the old, peeling, whitewashed walls so they can discover a profusion of architectural ornaments that meld into the facades like chameleons on the branches of trees. Some places are like people: their appearance is deceptive. Their true beauty only appears when you look beyond the first impression, and that beauty, far from fading with time, grows deeper, blossoming with the passing years.

Alice liked walking down the narrow streets of Cluny, especially the steep ones, like the Rue Sainte-Odile, the Rue Joséphine Desbois, and the Rue de la Barre. When she strolled along them, she enjoyed a perfectly wonderful view of the rooftops, a rhapsody of old tiles in varying shades of reds and browns, where steeples from the abbey and churches and the old Romanesque Tour des Fromages rose up, crowned in the distance by tree-covered hills, set against a sky that was often blue.

When she got to the end of the Rue de la République, Alice walked faster so as not to give in to the irresistible smell of warm brioche coming from Altmeyer's bakery. She passed the Fontaine aux Serpents. Its mossy, worn stonework did not catch the eye, and the motto high above it seemed meant for people who just happened to look up. Then they would discover its sumptuous gilt crown. FELIX CLUNIACI LOCUS IN QUO RIDENTI NATURAE SOLI PRESTANT CIVES. As a child, Alice thought that was some mysterious, magical saying. Many years later, she found out what it meant: CLUNY IS A HAPPY PLACE WHOSE INHABITANTS GO ABOUT THEIR BUSINESS IN NATURE'S SMILING SUNSHINE.


She thought back to what had happened to her the day before at Hermès, a quasi-mystical experience. Never in her life had she felt so good. She would give up everything she owned in exchange for the promise to live in that state until the end of her days, full of such joy.

She was ready to do anything to understand the enigmatic precepts of Jesus, starting with the most bizarre, the most incomprehensible ones, for she was now sure that they contained mysterious revelations, incredible hidden truths. And it was perhaps exactly because they were incredible that Jesus expressed himself in parables and not in an explicit way. Alice wanted to decipher those truths, whatever the cost.

She arrived in front of her elderly father's house and found the door open. She went inside and spotted him in the back garden, wearing a straw hat and working on his vegetables.

*"Chérie!"* he called out, turning around. "I was hoping you'd come."

She kissed him, then pulled up an old lime-green wrought-iron chair and sat down in the shade of an old walnut tree. A pair of pruning shears and a few cut roses sat on a round table in front of her. Her father remained standing, leaning on the handle of his spade.

"How are you?" he asked.

"Hot. The AC wasn't working on the train. And you?"

"Very well."

She suddenly realized that she normally wasn't very interested in him, only asked for his news out of habit and was content with the usual response. What if he was only being polite?

She calmly watched him as he took off his gardening gloves and put them down on the table. His features had been shaped by time and seemed to have retained the marks of his life, revealing both his joys and his suffering.

He disappeared and came back a moment later with a little vase of water for the roses.

"Is it very hard getting old?" she cautiously asked.

He smiled. "Aging brings its share of pain, of course, but despite everything, I'm much happier now than when I was twenty."

She frowned. "You never confided in me that your life was hard when you were young."

"It wasn't particularly."

Alice looked at him closely. "And you're happier now? Really?"

"Yes, truly."

"But...your eyesight is worse, your hearing as well. And you're always telling me that you can't remember things."

"True."

"That you search for words."

"Yes."

"That you have to rest after doing an hour of gardening."

"That's for sure."

"That even noise tires you out."

"All that is true, but it doesn't prevent me from being happier than when I was twenty."

Alice looked at him, perplexed. "And how do you explain that?'

He smiled, pulled up a chair, and put his straw hat down on the table. "Age has allowed me to free myself from my illusions, you see. To live in reality. And real life is happier than a life of illusions."

"You had illusions?"

"They have disappeared one by one as I've aged."

"I don't understand what you mean."

He took a deep breath. "With time, we are progressively freed from everything that made us unhappy when we were young: beauty, physical strength, success, and even intelligence, to a certain extent. All the handicaps we often have at twenty."

Alice was shocked: she suddenly realized that her father was losing his mind. It felt like a veil of sadness had been thrown over her. How could she not have noticed before? How could she not have seen the early signs? Too focused on herself, probably. She felt on the verge of tears. What if he had Alzheimer's?

"Papa...how...how do you feel right now?"

"I'm fine, why?"

"Can you...tell me again what you just said? I don't think you meant it."

"I was saying that time frees us from everything that made us unhappy when we were young: physical strength, beauty—"

"Papa...please, concentrate. You can't say things like that."

He started to laugh.

"Will you stop talking to me as if I were senile?"

Alice forced herself to smile, even though she knew that her concern could be spotted a mile away. "Papa, you know very well that it's not beauty, strength, and success that make people unhappy. It's...the complete opposite. Of course, I'm no longer in my twenties, but what prevents me from being really happy are my physical defects, my failures, and sometimes my lack of mental agility."

He smiled. "That is exactly what everyone believes at your age."

She sighed. "I've never admitted this to you, but when I was a teenager, I hated you for having given me the gene for a nose I thought was too big."

He burst out laughing. "Be thankful you didn't inherit my baldness!"

"Papa, there have been serious studies that show that good-looking people get work and high-level positions more easily. They have greater success. The same goes for height: the taller you are, the easier it is. That's been proven by sociologists, Papa—. Why are you laughing?"

"What's the use of getting high-level jobs or succeeding if you're unhappy?"

"But why are you insisting that beauty or other attributes everyone desires make you unhappy?"

He slowly leaned back in his chair. "Finally a good question."

Alice frowned, partly annoyed, partly reassured about her father's mental state. He looked at her and smiled.

"Well, go and get us the bottle of burgundy wine I put in the fridge for when you got here," he said. "Grab a few things to nibble on too."

Alice got up and came back a few minutes later with a well-stocked tray for their aperitif.

Her father took the bottle and uncorked it with his Swiss Army knife.

"A Philippe Valette Mâcon-Chaintré. He's passionate about natural wine! He's been making wine for twenty years and is an absolute master of the art."

He poured a little into his glass and swirled it around before bringing the glass to his nose. Alice saw his eyes sparkle with pleasure. He carefully tasted it, and a smile of satisfaction lit up his face.

"So delicate! So full-bodied! Those little hints of citrus..."

He poured them both some wine and raised his glass.

"To youth, whose advantages are also the main obstacles to happiness!"

Alice also took a sip of the wine, savoring the perfect balance of its many aromatic nuances.

Her father was now looking at the garden full of flowers, a secret garden like so many in Cluny, hidden behind houses that revealed only their seemingly insignificant facades to passersby.

When he started speaking again, his voice was quieter, more serious.

"In the past, when I was young, I thought getting older was very sad. To me it was the progressive loss of all our advantages. Everything that gave us our worth was gradually taken away as we got older."

He paused, and Alice tacitly agreed. She had the same view.

"And then," he continued, "because you can't stop time, I began to feel its effects. At first, you don't really realize it, and it's only when you chance upon a picture taken a few years earlier that you become aware of the...deterioration. At the time, it's a bit of a blow to the morale, but then you don't think about it anymore, and life goes on...and getting older does too."

He drank some wine. Alice did the same. Her throat was dry.

"And then one day, when I was about fifty, I realized an incredible thing: even though I was gradually losing everything that had been a source of pride to me, I was feeling better and better. It was illogical, incomprehensible, and not at all what I had expected. That's when a difficult event threw my life into turmoil."

"You lost your job."

"Yes. At the time when my capabilities were starting to taper off a little, I suddenly lost my job, and that was a shock. In those days, unemployment was relatively rare. Many people spent their entire careers in the same company. We didn't have an official guarantee of a job for life, but in practice, that's what it came down to."

He drank some more wine.

"Once the shock passed, I was angry. Then I felt very sad, but the sadness also ended up vanishing. I wasn't overly upset about it because I had confidence in my ability to find another job: someone always needs a business manager somewhere. And, of course, pottery manufacturing was a dying industry in the area, but I knew my skills would be transferable elsewhere. In the meantime, your mother's salary and my unemployment insurance were enough to keep the family going. Nevertheless, I remained unemployed long enough to realize something incredible."

"What?"

"It's difficult to describe. But...I discovered that I wasn't my work."

"That you weren't your work?"

"I went on living despite my professional failure. I went on living despite the lack of a job. Up until then, my work had been such a source of pride to me. Being a business manager was my life."

"Isn't that fairly normal? When you like your work, when you are fulfilled by what you do, you devote your life to it."

115

"Yes, but it went further than that: I felt I existed only *through* my work. In my mind, I was a business manager, and in hindsight, even if I didn't realize it at the time, I was nothing else. I also wasn't a very good father..."

"That's in the past, Papa."

"I identified completely with my professional role, you see, and when that role was taken away, it was as if a large part of myself had been taken away, if not my very reason to live. I suffered enormously, and then...then I ended up discovering that my life was not limited to that role, that I wasn't my job but just a man who was doing a job."

"I see..."

"And if I defined myself through my profession, it was because it gave me a great sense of pride."

Alice looked at him, deep in thought. "Just like your strength, physical appearance, intellect, and sophistication in your youth."

He agreed.

Alice ate an olive and took a deep breath. The countless white flowers of the mock orange bushes gave off a wonderful, delicate scent. Her father looked at her.

"I realized that you become attached to what makes you proud, to the point of defining yourself by it and believing that you are whatever is the source of that pride. And the more you believe that, the further away you find yourself from what you really are. Pride is a product of illusions, the fuel of a machine that pushes you away from your true nature, a diminisher of identity."

*A diminisher of identity...*

*That's where the problem truly lies,* thought Alice. *Defining ourselves through one of our attributes diminishes the extent of who we are.*

"And the progressive decline of beauty, of physical and mental skills, helps to detach us from those false identities, is that it?"

"To those who accept the decline."

"What do you mean?"

"I have the impression that certain people who identify too much with those things can desperately resist and deny their aging, hiding it from others and perhaps even from themselves. They don't realize that by clutching on to things that were no more than illusions, they are missing out on allowing who they really are to surface. By thinking they're saving their identity, they are losing it."

Alice had a strange feeling listening to those last words, as if she had already heard or read them somewhere. Jesus, perhaps. Jesus must have said something similar.

"Have you ever talked to anyone about all this? For example, the people you know who might have forgotten who they are?"

"It's not easy. You can't fight against illusions, and no one likes having them pointed out."

Alice made a face and shrugged her shoulders. "If a friend prevented me from deluding myself, he would be a true friend."

Her father seemed touched by her remark and had a faraway look in his eyes for a long moment, as if he was going through his memories.

"When I think about it," he admitted, "several of my friends probably defined themselves through their professions. They gave the impression that they only existed through their work. Like I did before being unemployed helped me to put it all in perspective."

"But I imagine they're no longer young enough to work, so how are they doing now?"

Her father stared at her for a moment, as if hesitant to continue. His eyes were suddenly tinged with sadness.

"They all died very soon after they retired."

# 16

"Are you sure about what you're saying, Madame de Sirdegault?"

The bishop had been so certain he didn't have to worry about that kind of thing.

He saw her acquiesce, eyes half closed, dazzled by the sun that shone through the tall, small-paned windows of the bishop's palace. Despite everything, she remained a very dignified woman with a serious expression, her head held high. She sat up so straight that you might have thought she was wearing a corset—as stiff as the cross with the large ruby she wore around her neck. He couldn't remember ever having seen her smile. Or perhaps she had: before her divorce.

He looked outside. The baroness had parked her old English racing-green Jaguar right below his window.

"You believe that Father Jeremy is being influenced by a young woman?"

"It's obvious, Your Grace. In any case, I'm only warning you about this as a friend, so that you're not the last to know."

"You are too kind. Does that mean others have noticed?"

"Without a doubt."

"Many others?"

"Enough."

The bishop sighed. Fortunately, the baroness regularly kept him informed about what was going on in the parish. Knowledge was the key to power.

"Is she...pretty?"

Madame de Sirdegault looked at him sternly. "I'm not in the habit of judging the physical attributes of young women, Your Grace."

The bishop stared at her for a few moments. She stared back without blinking.

"And how do you think the others find her?"

"People say she's beautiful."

The bishop nodded. *People say she's beautiful.* Father Jeremy was perhaps still too young to know how to resist a temptress. A temptress who was getting involved in things that were none of her business. They were headed for a scandal. And in its current state, the church could do without that. Especially in his diocese.

\*  \*  \*

When she opened the front door that afternoon to get a file she'd forgotten, Alice immediately smelled the warm steam of the iron.

"Are you here already, Rosetta?" she called out.

"I got here early," Rosetta replied from the bedroom.

Alice put down her things and opened the closet in the hall.

119

She took out a large present wrapped in Christmas paper with Santa Clauses on it, the remains of what she'd bought a few months before to wrap up her nephews' toys.

She went into the bedroom, walked over to the cleaner, and handed her the package.

"This is for you, Rosetta. I was in Burgundy this weekend, and I brought this back for you."

Rosetta seemed surprised. "For me? That's very nice of you."

Alice smiled.

Rosetta took the package, which she nearly dropped.

"It's really heavy!"

She put it down on the ironing board, next to the iron, which gave out a small burst of steam. She started to unwrap it by scratching at the Scotch tape with her index finger, but it wouldn't come off, so she ended up tearing off the paper.

"Oh!"

Alice smiled at her. "I thought you'd like it."

Rosetta turned as red as a newborn baby who's been plunged into a cold baptismal font in the dead of winter.

"Thanks very much," she stammered, without looking at Alice. She was staring at the large package of laundry detergent she was holding in her hands.

\*　　\*　　\*

An hour later, Alice was back at the office on the fifty-third floor of the Montparnasse Tower, sitting comfortably in her large swivel chair turned toward the window that overlooked Paris. Leaning back slightly and facing the immense sky, she thought back to her experience at Hermès and her conversation with her father the past weekend.

Okay, she existed independent of her profession, her appearance, her intellect, and the approval of others. *That* she could understand and accept. In a certain way, it was almost obvious. But then why did she pay so much attention to her image? Why did she feel devalued in the presence of any woman more beautiful than she was, or a more brilliant colleague, or a more sophisticated friend? Why, whenever she met someone in a high position, did she feel pressure to let them know she was a consultant and to make herself seem important? Why did she need to do that if her life and her true worth didn't depend on those things?

At Hermès, she had deliberately quashed her self-esteem, swallowed her pride, allowed herself to be ignored, despised. And strangely, that had led her to a feeling of joy, of unparalleled inspiration. So there *was* an existence beyond the way we see ourselves, present ourselves, beyond the way others see us.

Alice took a deep breath and looked up at the blue sky. All that was very vague, very mysterious. She sensed she was touching upon something essential, primordial. She was trying to find her way, almost blindly, through unknown territory.

Suddenly, an idea came to her. Her friend Toby Collins could shed some light on this for her.

She picked up the phone, dialed his cell number, and waited, restlessly, as it continued to ring. Outside, along the large window, she could see the window washer's platform cable vibrating. He must be a few stories below.

"Toby?"

"Yes."

"Toby, it's Alice, from Paris. How are you?"

"Alice! My God! It's so nice to hear from you!"

Alice couldn't stop herself from smiling when she heard the warmth in her friend's voice. She asked for his news, then explained the thoughts that were motivating her.

"The ego," said Toby. "You're interested in the ego."

"The ego?"

"Yes."

"I don't know. I occasionally use the term in conversation, like everyone does, but without knowing exactly what it means."

"It's actually quite simple. We don't really know who we are, because who we are is too abstract, so we tend to lump together our being with a certain number of tangible things: our physical appearance, attributes, intelligence, profession, or even the roles we give ourselves."

"Roles?"

"Yes, without actually realizing it, we can adopt a certain role and stick to it more and more: the role of the cool guy, the active woman, the unloved introvert, the tough guy who's a little macho, the sweet and kind person, et cetera. There are an endless number of them, of course."

"Is that a problem?"

"Not in itself, but it is limiting. We're not *just* our profession, our beauty, our intelligence, or the role we've taken on. But because we tend to define ourselves by it, somewhere inside, we necessarily feel that it's somewhat feeble. And then fear sets in: fear of not being *sufficiently* what we believe we are. Fear we're not beautiful *enough,* intelligent *enough,* gifted *enough,* competent *enough,* not good *enough* at the profession or role we're trying to define ourselves by."

"I see."

"We start believing that we will be valued for those attributes, without realizing that they are, in fact, relatively external to ourselves, or, in any case, secondary. But since who I am is difficult to define, and even hard to feel, well, it leads me to clutch on more and more to the elements I believe define me, to believe that they *are* me, and I insist on defending them against any decline. I feel any criticism about my physical appearance, my ideas, or my skills as a criticism of who I am, as if my own worth had been questioned. So then I feel wounded or cut to the quick, and depending on my personality, I either disappear and withdraw into my illusionary self or I strongly reject the criticism and perhaps even launch a counterattack to protect myself."

"I've actually realized that myself."

"There you go."

Alice thought she could detect slight frustration in Toby's voice. Perhaps he was busy and she was bothering him? Another two minutes and she'd let him go.

"And what is the link to the ego?"

He remained silent for a moment.

"The 'ego' is what we call that mental construction around the idea we have of ourselves. It's a false identity that, in a certain way, inhibits our true nature. And yet we hang on to it and are prepared to do anything to defend it. The ego can be seen as a part of ourselves that takes control, expresses itself in our place, and especially would like to exist more and more within us."

"And . . . is there a way around it?"

There was another moment of dead air on the line. When Toby started talking again, Alice found his voice colder.

"Tell me, Alice, with all these questions . . . are you coming to me as a friend or a consultant?"

"Um . . . it's the same thing . . . isn't it?"

"No, Alice, it's not the same thing."

"Okay, well, what's the difference, then?"

Another brief silence.

"Five hundred dollars, my dear."

Stopped in her tracks, Alice mumbled something. The conversation came to a sudden end, and she hung up, disappointed, her heart heavy.

Outside the window, the Senegalese window cleaner imitated her baffled expression before looking sorry for her.

She tried to smile back at him. Was he really nice and funny or had he adopted the role of the nice and funny window cleaner? Her disappointment in Toby made her mistrustful.

She sighed. Had she ever truly been Toby's friend? During the seminars, every time there had been a break, she had done everything possible to establish, then maintain, their relationship. Why? When all was said and done, did she really like him?

Every question she asked brought its own answer, and Alice quickly saw the obvious: she had been mainly flattered to be the friend of a celebrity, as if she were also defined by her relationships. *I mix with people who have worth, therefore I have worth.* And hadn't she subtly made it known to the people around her that she was Collins's friend? Ego again, most likely.

Collins, the high priest of personal development. Still, he had helped her enormously—she had to recognize that, not turn her back on him because she was annoyed. It was thanks to him that she had learned to love herself, have confidence in herself, free herself from her doubts and fears. He himself had so much confidence, was so self-assured, so embodied success.

On the other side of the window, the Senegalese man was carefully doing his work. They glanced at each other again, and he gave her such a kindly, sincere smile that it warmed her heart.

As for Collins, what if the goal in life was more than simply being content with yourself and knowing how to manage things in your own self-interest?

She sighed as she dreamily watched the window washer's movements, regular, very efficient. She herself was in the process of cleaning the distorting lenses through which she viewed her life.

She loved the window washer's empathetic, positive, humane

attitude. No, that wasn't a role. He was being himself; she would swear to it. He seemed down-to-earth and direct, and somewhere inside her, she envied that straightforwardness. He wouldn't go to the trouble of asking himself existential questions!

She then realized that, nevertheless, she felt—how could she put it?—a little superior to him. She who had philosophical concerns and was trying to raise her level of spirituality. She was angry at herself for having that feeling and suddenly was aware of the enormous trap into which she was about to fall: the person seeking liberation from her ego and increased spirituality was risking…seeing her ego take over this process and identifying with it!

It reminded her of a funny cartoon by Voutch: a person dressed as a Buddhist monk climbing up a mountain while saying, "I want to learn humility! I want to become the number-one *world champion* of humility!"

She turned again toward the window, but the platform was rising to the higher floors, leaving her alone in her luxurious office on the fifty-third floor of the Montparnasse Tower, as the window cleaner rose toward the heavens.

# 17

THE PHONE RANG. IT WAS PAUL.

"I'm calling from the house, darling."

"What are you doing at home at this hour? It's not even six o'clock."

"I just got out of a meeting that was nearby. I didn't want to have to cross Paris again during rush hour."

"Great, then you can take care of Théo tonight! I've been invited to a gallery opening after work and thought I wouldn't be able to go!"

"Okay," he said, without much enthusiasm. "Will you be getting home late?"

"I'll just have a quick look around, since I've actually been invited out for once."

"Okay. But I have to tell you something. Get this: Just as I got home, I ran straight into Rosetta, who was leaving. And you know what she was carrying? An enormous package of detergent!"

"Uh..."

"I remembered how stressed you were about her pilfering. I caught her in the act, and it was too good an opportunity to miss. I fired her on the spot. In any case, that was the best possible solution: we won't have to pay for her vacation! So it's over and done with. Do you feel better?"

"No, wait—"

"She protested, as you can imagine, but her story would never hold up. She's finished. We got rid of her."

"Actually—"

"I'll tell you anyway, it will make you laugh: she insisted that it was a gift from you, a souvenir from Burgundy! I stopped myself from laughing so I could continue to pretend to be offended!"

"Paul, she was telling the truth."

A long silence on the other end of the line.

"I don't understand you at all, Alice."

Alice suddenly felt very alone. How could she explain it to him?

"Alice, what's all this craziness?"

"Well... you're going to laugh at me, but... I just wanted to follow Jesus's teaching to see what happened. The one that says: 'And if anyone wants to take your shirt, hand over your coat as well.'"

Silence.

"You've become very strange, Alice."

*     *     *

An hour later, Alice pushed opened the door to the Mag Daniels Gallery, an art gallery on the Rue de Seine that was very in vogue. There were already a fair number of people inside. A Who's Who of the Saint-Germain crowd seemed to be there, all holding glasses of champagne, and Alice felt flattered to have been invited.

She crossed the gallery amid animated conversations, the scent of expensive perfumes, and sophisticated outfits worn with great nonchalance. At the back of the room, the artist was perched on the edge of a table, dressed all in black. He was listening to a woman who was probably telling him how much she admired his work. Alice took a glass of champagne and made her way through the glittering crowd to try to see the paintings. The guests seemed more interested in their own analysis of the works than the works themselves. Among them, a man in his fifties was strutting around like a peacock, talking louder than everyone else, and putting on airs. People seemed to be paying attention and even flattering him.

Alice walked around the exhibition. The artist was consistent in his style: his paintings were all large and composed of a single dark background color—blue, brown, or black—and a series of vertical, parallel lines of varying thickness in turquoise, lemon yellow, and even raspberry pink. They weren't unpleasant—they looked like stylized, colorful bar codes.

Alice picked up little bits of conversations here and there, and it was entertaining, a real little theater of smugness. It all ended up—despite everything—resembling a barnyard: this one meowed his credentials, that one chirped with self-importance, another cooed inspired commentary, yet another stamped the ground with criticisms meant to elevate himself above the person he was destroying. And when someone in the group stood out because they had a few ideas on the history of art, the others nodded in a knowing way: in the kingdom of morons, the pedants ruled.

She walked by the woman who was talking to the artist and overheard her telling him about her own paintings.

The dance of the vanities was in full swing. The ego was everywhere, ruling supreme over the evening. Alice had the impression that absolutely no one was simply being themselves. They were all putting on airs, playing a role, practicing their mannerisms, facial expressions, and remarks, and pretending to be moved. They hid behind their egos to the point of disappearing altogether. As if they no longer existed, as if they were . . . dead, replaced by some parasite that had invaded their minds and taken possession of their gestures, their speech, their souls.

Alice thought of Jesus. She hadn't understood when he had used the term "death" in sayings where it seemed out of place, as in "Whoever hears my word . . . has crossed over from death to life." She remembered having found that ridiculous—she was very much alive even before hearing his words.

But what if Jesus meant the same thing as her, seeing people devoured by their egos as dead? And besides, thinking about it, Jesus himself seemed free of all ego, even if he never used the word. Others called him the Messiah, a Prophet, the Son of God, or even King of the Jews. Not him. He never gave himself any title at all. He simply called himself the "son of Adam," sometimes translated as the "son of man"—like all men! It was as if he refused to identify himself with anything at all, refused to be considered important. Or as if he wanted to lead by example.

The more illustrations that came to mind, the more Alice felt troubled.

Healing the sick! Most of the time, Jesus accomplished this alone, with no one watching, asking the crowd to leave, and even demanding that no one mention it, that no one repeat what they had seen. He obviously rejected fame and glory.

Alice saw the link with her own experience at Hermès, with the enlightenment she had felt when trying to put into practice his saying "Blessed are you when people insult you, persecute you." What if Jesus meant that you find happiness when you free yourself from your ego?

"Normally, pretty women are introduced to me. The old ways are dying out. What's your name, my dear?"

Alice looked up. It was the man she'd seen strutting around a few minutes earlier.

"Alice."

He passed a lecherous look across her breasts, then her stomach, then her crotch. She felt like a piece of meat.

"What a delightful name. What do you do for a living, my dear?"

She hesitated for a few seconds, then looked him straight in the eye.

"I'm a window washer."

"Oh, oh!" He chuckled, incredulous.

"Why are you laughing?"

She saw his expression change from disbelief to doubt as he sized her up more closely.

"No, no, I'm not laughing."

He gave her an embarrassed, slightly condescending smile. She had the feeling that he was about to turn and walk away.

"What about you? Who are you?"

After the first instant, when she had felt demeaned by saying that she had quite a menial job, Alice now was enjoying—how could she put it—a kind of freedom. She had nothing to lose, no status to defend, no role to play that would correspond to the image she usually projected as a PR consultant.

He gave a little scornful laugh. "You're probably the only person here who doesn't know, my dear. I'm an art critic."

One of the women guests, who had been buzzing around him like a fly, came to stand next to Alice, smiling at him: "He's the one who calls the shots in the art market."

"So that's what you do," Alice said, looking him straight in the eye. "But I asked you who you are, not what you do."

130

"Well...but..." He seemed disconcerted by her words.

He raised his chin higher and higher, as if he were trying to hoist himself above her.

"You don't know who you are?"

"But...I am Antoine Dupont!" he said in a self-righteous tone of voice. "Everyone knows me."

His fans agreed.

Alice looked around the room. No one was interested in the paintings anymore.

Alone, forgotten, slumped in a baroque armchair upholstered in fluorescent colors at the back of the gallery, the painter was licking his wounds and playing at being the misunderstood artist.

Alice made a face. "And if your parents had given you a different first name, or if they themselves had inherited another last name, you wouldn't be Antoine Dupont. But would you be someone else?"

He was becoming more and more disconcerted.

"No...of course not," he finally stammered.

Alice stared straight at him.

"So who are you, really, in the end, if you aren't Antoine Dupont?"

# 18

*When you unclothe yourselves and are not ashamed, and take your garments and trample on them, then . . . you will no longer be afraid.*

Alice closed her Bible, whose *Civil Code* cover was partly torn, and took a deep breath.

She remembered having laughed a lot the first time she read that sentence.

Now she could read a unique message between the lines. Jesus seemed to be saying that it was shame that led us to wear clothing, and that by learning to take it off, we would be liberated from fear. But Jesus didn't walk around stark naked! So the word "clothing" couldn't be taken literally. It was surely a metaphor, like the ones Jesus often used, and Alice couldn't help but think it referred to the ego. "Clothing" probably meant the false identities we wore like veils that masked who we were, the false images we assigned ourselves by identifying with a role, a profession, our appearance, or our skills. And Jesus gave a reason for that: shame.

A little farther away, Rachid was at his desk, completely absorbed in his computer screen. Alice, lost in thought, turned toward the window and looked out into the distance, beyond the clouds that filled the Parisian sky.

Shame.

Of course.

It's shame over who we naturally are, beyond anything we can do or reveal to the world, it's the fear of never being *good enough* that leads us to take on roles, embellish our abilities, and defend them tooth and nail, because they protect us from the nakedness of our identity, which we believe—and wrongly so—not to be good enough.

Alice took another deep breath.

Jesus promised that by freeing ourselves from all those artifices, we would be free of fear. Perhaps because we would then realize the value—the infinite value—of our being, without needing to do or display anything. To be without pretending. Just to be.

Isn't that what she had experienced at Hermès?

She smiled when she remembered that in mythology, Hermes, Zeus's messenger, was most notably the link between the world of the gods and the earthly world.

A few years ago she had visited Greece and had been very intrigued to learn that there was a second maxim on the pediment of the Temple of Apollo in Delphi. The entire world had learned "Know thyself," but everyone seemed to have forgotten "Everything in moderation." She'd never heard anyone talk about it.

At the time, that saying had struck her as mysterious. Today, she understood it better. "Know thyself" and "Everything in moderation" invited people to become themselves again and not see themselves as who they are not.

Outside the office window, the clouds began to slowly drift away.

After discovering the similarities between Jesus and Lao Tzu, Alice could now see how close they were to the dictums of the wise men of ancient Greece, several centuries before Christ. Everything seemed to converge.

There must be a kind of cosmic truth, some universal wisdom about being freed from the ego that spread across centuries and continents but without managing to reach people. As if humans unconsciously filtered the messages intended for them, to avoid hearing the ones that questioned their egos.

At this point in her discoveries, Alice suspected it was perhaps her ego that was responsible for most of her personal problems and day-to-day difficulties.

She had never perceived that wisdom through Christianity, despite Jesus's messages, which she had only just begun to decipher. To be fair, she had started setting foot in church only a few months ago! She couldn't really consider herself an expert. But when she thought of her Catholic friends, the spirituality of the least observant often seemed to boil down to a few minor restrictions, like not eating meat on Good Friday. The spirituality of the most observant involved a lot of restrictions—not to make love before marriage, not to commit the sins of gluttony, sloth, envy, or wrath—which led them to feel guilty for just about everything!

She hadn't seen anything in their practices related to liberation from the ego. It mainly resembled a moral code. She found it difficult to understand how that could raise someone's level of spirituality.

Alice felt that liberation from the ego was the key to something else that was more spiritually beneficial, like a door that opened to another world—a world she had only just begun to explore.

She wanted to go further in that direction, but how? She was blocked by the limitations of her plan: putting Jesus's words into practice to experience them herself had worked until now, but how could she experiment with precepts like "Happy are the poor in spirit" or abstaining from sin? Play the fool for a month and you'll lose your job. Two months of chastity and you'll end up divorced.

*The poor in spirit* . . . Alice recalled the very similar expression used by Lao Tzu: "simple of spirit." In the end, she had not made much effort to shed light on these troubling parallels. Her disappointing encounter with the Taoist monk had thwarted her enthusiasm. Perhaps she should have continued on in that direction. Perhaps that ancient philosophy contained the key to understanding Jesus's messages.

"You don't know any Taoists, by any chance, do you?"

Rachid looked up. "Never met any."

"Or know someone else who does?"

He frowned. "Um . . . No, I don't . . ."

"Or know someone who knows someone who knows any?" she said, laughing.

"No. The only person who comes to mind is Raphaël Duvernet, the expert on Eastern religions."

"Raphaël Duvernet? Isn't he dead?"

Rachid burst out laughing. "In a way, yes! But he's still around, I think. I asked him to speak at a company conference just before he fell from grace. I have his contact details if you want them."

A few years before, the expert in question had been caught up in a scandal while at the height of his fame, a time when his books on spirituality sold in the millions and he was the darling of the media. His wife at the time, probably frustrated that he cheated on her with everyone in sight, had revealed everything: Raphaël Duvernet, respected and seen as virtually a mystic, was egotistical and neurotic, tyrannical with his entourage, prepared to go to any lengths to appear on television, and, to top it all off, he used ghostwriters to make sure he published two books a year and thus cornered the market on East Asian wisdom.

"And what's more, he lives near you," Rachid added.

"Near Bastille?"

"No, in Burgundy."

"You're kidding."

"Not at all. Monsieur has a château. The life of an ascetic, don't you know."

The following weekend, Alice was crossing the drawbridge of an enormous medieval château, hidden away on an estate with hundred-year-old trees, near a village in the Mâcon region, twenty or so kilometers from Cluny. She walked under a kind of archway and found herself in a garden surrounded by a horse-shoe-shaped outer wall. A few rows of poorly kept box hedges surrounded the flower beds. It was meant to resemble a French garden, but the grass was too long.

Alice headed for a large studded door made of old oak that looked like the main entrance. Since there was no bell, she lifted the heavy cast-iron door knocker and banged it three times.

She almost expected a knight in armor to open it, but it was only an unassuming woman who looked tired and sad. A servant? A member of the family?

"Come in. He's in the wine cellar," she said in a timid voice after Alice had introduced herself. "Go on, it's that way."

She pointed to a dark spiral staircase that seemed to plunge down into the bowels of the fortress.

"I'd rather wait until he comes back up. If you would just let him know..."

The woman looked over at a man whose body and features appeared emaciated. At first, Alice hadn't noticed him standing in the shadows. He slightly shrugged his shoulders without replying, his eyes glazed over.

"He probably won't come upstairs soon," the woman said with a sigh. "You'd be better off going downstairs to see him."

Alice hardly wanted to do that.

She hesitated. Her hosts gave her a suspicious look. Their faces were colorless and their eyes sunken.

She slowly started down the stone staircase, whose steps were unevenly worn by the passage of time. The deeper she descended, the damper the air became. Once at the bottom of the stairs, she continued down a long passageway with vaulted ceilings of gray stone, dimly lit by lamps resembling the old tarnished copper lanterns that were once used on horse-drawn carriages.

The passageway ended in an immense wine cellar, also with vaulted ceilings but where the light from stately wrought-iron wall sconces created a warmer atmosphere, despite the stone walls and dirt floor. Dozens and dozens of large barrels were lined up in rows. At the back, an immense Persian carpet covered the floor, and on it stood an oak wine-tasting table surrounded by rather unexpected Louis XIII armchairs covered in red velvet. About thirty glasses were set out on the table.

Sitting in one of the armchairs was the famous Raphaël Duvernet, hair unkempt and white beard badly trimmed, holding a glass of red wine. In silence, he looked her up and down with his dark eyes.

She had seen him dozens of times on television a few years ago, so it was strange to see him in the flesh. His wrinkles had deepened, carving out furrows in his rather reddish, puffy face. She found him very stern, but behind his harshness she sensed a kind of distress.

Alice cleared her throat as she walked toward him, all smiles.

"I'm Al—"

"And I'm Raph," he grumbled, looking away.

Alice tried to keep smiling. "You must have been told I was coming and that I needed some clarification about—"

"Tasting the Burgundy marc brandy..." He had said it in a grim voice.

"No, Eastern religions."

"You've come to the wrong place."

"I'd like to understand certain Taoist concepts..."

He shrugged his shoulders, staring at the glass he slowly turned in his hand. After a long pause, he let out an almost inaudible sigh. "Why the hell would you give a damn about that?"

Alice felt the anger rising within her and tried to remain calm despite her raging desire to punch him in the face.

*Flatter him to soften him up.*

"Listen. I know that you're an expert on spirituality."

He scowled slightly. It looked like a tortured smile. "I've gone from the spiritual to the spirits."

Alice bit her lip. This wasn't going to be easy. "Well, then, offer me a glass of wine."

He seemed surprised. He turned toward her and stared at her for a long time in silence.

Then he made the effort to get up and lean over the table, inspecting the numerous glasses. Alice realized they were all dirty.

"Nadine!" he shouted. "A glass for Mademoiselle."

"Madame."

"Madame," he hissed after a moment.

There was little chance that Nadine had heard him call, so a few seconds later, Alice was surprised to hear footsteps coming down the stairs and along the passageway. She recognized the woman who had greeted her. Nadine put a glass down on the table and slipped out again.

Meanwhile, Duvernet had taken a bottle of sparkling wine and uncorked it. The sharp popping noise echoed throughout the wine cellar. After filling two glasses, he took one and held it up to see it, then sniffed it.

"A Tripoz," he said. "Brut. Pure. The perfect balance of aromas. Beautiful!"

He spoke in a husky voice, in a tone that was both depressed and somewhat aggressive. He handed her the second glass.

*Be patient.*

*Tame the beast.*

"The aroma is very fine," she said.

"The bubbles are unbelievably delicate!" His gruff tone of voice contrasted with the finesse he was describing.

She took a sip. She lacked the imagination to continue a discussion about wine. "I admit it is exceptional."

"You see?"

"Yes, very good. You're right."

"Ah . . ."

"Have you been drinking this wine for a long time?"

"Only discovered it recently."

They fell silent.

*Don't allow the silence to continue. Keep going.*

"An excellent discovery," she said.

"Oh yes, an amazing find."

"Definitely."

139

"It takes years of work," he said, "decades, to succeed at making a wine like this!"

"Yes, and great intelligence as well, I imagine. It would take someone who wasn't simple of spirit."

"Definitely."

Alice took a deep breath and launched in. "Simple of spirit . . . I always wondered why Lao Tzu said 'My heart is the heart of someone simple of spirit.' That's strange, isn't it?"

She waited, on edge, for his reply. For a long time.

"In my opinion, tea wasn't the only thing he ever drank."

Alice repressed her desire to shake Duvernet like a plum tree.

"Rice wine, perhaps?" she said, trying to laugh.

"That's disgusting stuff."

She chuckled out of politeness, then waited a moment. "What do you think he meant?"

"That he probably had the goodness of a village idiot. Sweet and stupid."

Alice felt her frustration growing. Her strategy wasn't working. She was wasting time with this guy. She tried to breathe to stay calm.

In vain.

"And when are you going to stop taking me for a moron?" she asked.

"When you stop taking me for one."

They locked eyes for the first time and stared at each other intensely.

"So from one moron to another, we can finally clink glasses."

He seemed to appreciate what she said, and their glasses banged together so hard that she thought they might break.

She took a sip. The Tripoz was truly delicious.

"Now you're going to answer my questions. This is important to me."

He let out a heavy sigh. "What exactly do you want to know?"

His tone of voice had changed. It had gone from aggressive to hollow.

"There are a few expressions and concepts that escape me, and I want to understand. Like the idea of 'simple of spirit.'"

He took a long drink of wine, admired its golden color, then began speaking slowly. His statements were precise, but talking seemed to take an enormous amount out of him, and he frequently paused between sentences.

"When Lao Tzu speaks of the spirit, he means the mind. On this question, Taoism is akin to Hinduism and Buddhism. They all call for a liberation from the mind, the cerebral. The cerebral is the incessant thinking that takes ascendency over the heart and body, to the detriment of intuition, instinct, and the awareness of being."

"The awareness of being?"

A few seconds of silence.

"When you are in your mind, it's a little as if you are no longer inhabiting your body, no longer listening to your heart, no longer feeling your existence. You are interpreting reality, and most often distorting it. You assign intentions to others that are not theirs; you project your fears, your problems, your doubts and expectations. You think about events instead of living them. Eastern religions invite us to free ourselves from the hold of the mind so we can feel things as they are, in the present moment, whereas the cerebral knows only the past and the future."

*Only the past and the future . . .*

"I don't understand the link you're making between the mind and time."

He looked at her for a moment and took another deep breath. Dealing with these subjects was difficult for him.

"Your mind interprets the event that is happening, or the

141

words that someone is saying, depending on your knowledge, your personal history, and your beliefs and convictions about yourself, other people, and the rest of the world. All those things come from the past. And if the present makes you feel afraid, it's because you are mentally projecting your interpretations from the past onto an imaginary future. That is how the mind cuts you off from the present."

"And Lao Tzu compared himself to someone simple of spirit because he had freed himself of his mind, is that it?"

Silence.

"Apparently," said Duvernet.

Jesus had said, "Happy are the poor in spirit." He was talking about the same thing, undeniably. And not about the spirit of poverty, as the Parisian priest had told her.

Duvernet took the bottle of sparkling wine and poured them both another glass. She didn't stop him.

"Is there ... Is there a link, somewhere, between the mind and ... the ego?"

"The ego is fundamentally the fruit of fear: fear of not being *enough,* of not having value, especially in the eyes of others. And unfounded fears are typically the product of a mental process. It is also our thoughts that lead us to take ourselves for what we are not: the mind pushes the ego to take on different roles. The mind feeds the ego."

He took a drink of wine before adding, "Buddhism asks us to detach ourselves from those damned roles." He had said the word "damned" with anger in his voice.

Buddhist detachment. "I've heard people talk about that, but it always seemed problematic to me. It gives the impression that you have to live in a state of detachment, without feeling anything about what is happening. But as for me, I have no desire whatsoever to live detached from my husband, my little boy, the people I love. I have no desire whatsoever to be indifferent to them, or insensitive. Obviously, if I were detached from them, I would suffer less if something bad happened to them. But if everything happens normally, then I don't see how I would be happier—quite the opposite!"

A new silence.

"You shouldn't take everything so literally," he continued in his slow, serious tone of voice. "In Buddhist detachment, it is especially important to understand that we manage to free ourselves from the hold the ego has on us. Your ego clings on to everything that gives you value but which is not you: the roles you play, the beautiful things you own, your most flattering attributes. And, of course..."—he paused for a moment, then lowered his voice to mutter under his breath—"your fucking successes."

*Don't take everything so literally...*

Alice recalled Jesus's response to the rich young man who came to see him for advice. Jesus told him, "Sell everything you have and give to the poor, and you will have treasure in heaven." Alice had found that advice strange: how would getting rid of all his possessions bring anything at all to that man? Don't the majority of people work their entire lives to manage to buy a house and a few other things? But, in fact, Jesus's advice might be in keeping with Buddhist detachment. Perhaps he had felt that the man was *attached* to his worldly goods, and it was that attachment that caused the problem. Maybe Jesus's message meant not that it was necessary to own nothing to be happy but that one shouldn't be *attached* to material possessions.

"The other day," Duvernet continued, "in Mâcon, I saw someone jump the light at an intersection in his BMW while another person, coming from the right, ran his red light. They didn't hit each other hard; the BMW just had a dent in its bumper. They both stopped and the guy got out, he was in his forties, and when he saw his BMW dented, he started to cry. No one was hurt, not even the slightest scratch, just a bit of bent metal, and the guy started bawling like a kid. Truly. I walked over to him and asked, 'Are you hurt?'

"'No.'

"'Do you have insurance?'

"'Yes.'

"'Will your premium go up?'

"'No, it will be okay.' His chin was quivering as he spoke.

"Well, in fact, it was his ego that was bawling, because his car was like an extension of himself. It contributed to his personal worth, and he must have felt he lived through it. In the end, it was a little bit of himself that had been damaged, so he was crying."

"Attachment to material possessions leads me to another question I wanted to ask you—"

"How long is this going to take?"

"We'll be done soon!"

"Thank goodness for that."

"I'd like to know how you feel about sin, about giving in to temptation."

As she spoke, he had been pouring himself another glass of wine. Now he gave her a dark look, the bottle in his hand.

"Are you screwing around with me?"

"Not at all! Lao Tzu talks about desire several times, and I wondered if there was a parallel between that and the notion of sin in Christianity."

He continued to stare at her in a very mistrustful way for a few seconds, then calmly picked up his glass and slowly raised it, seeming to admire the color of the wine. He breathed in its aroma once more.

"Desire in Eastern religions leads back to the ego. It is the ego that desires an object, a promotion, more money, or whatever else, because the ego is always trying to reinforce itself, increase its worth with the object of desire. Through what we desire, we subconsciously seek to augment our identity, or rather what we feel is our identity. In fact, we tend to be confused about who we are, so we don't know exactly how to go about being more ourselves. So we desire things in an attempt to exist a little more thanks to them. When you desire a piece of clothing, a car, or anything else, you subconsciously believe that the clothing or car will add something to who you are, will make you special, interesting, valuable. In short, it will reinforce your identity. It's an illusion, of course, and Eastern religions like Taoism, Buddhism, and Hinduism ask us to free ourselves from desire."

"But why? What's the problem?"

"Desire quickly leads to slavery. Since it is based on an illusion, to reinforce your identity, the object of desire doesn't bring what you are seeking, so it's an endless quest: you continually desire new things, things that never bring you what you are looking for. That's why Lao Tzu said, 'There is no worse disaster than the desire to possess.' And 'The holy man has no desire other than to have no desires.'"

*Desire quickly leads to slavery* . . . Alice recalled what Jesus had said that had made her smile: "Everyone who sins is a slave to sin."

"And in your opinion, is there a link with the concept of sin in Christianity?"

He sighed. "These mythologies really have nothing to do with one another, so it's very difficult to make comparisons."

"Mythologies?"

"Um . . . I meant religions. A Freudian slip: read Campbell, the famous American expert on mythology, and you will understand that the Bible is rather similar to mythology."

Alice wrote down the name. "But what if we tried a comparison anyway?"

"Christians see sin as an offense against God, as disobedience to divine law, which could lead to hell after death. Unbelievably stupid. Jesus spoke Aramaic, and years later, his apostles reported his words when writing the Gospels. Except that they wrote in ancient Greek, so they were translating Jesus's words from Aramaic to Greek. Then the ancient Greek was translated into our modern languages. Several specialists in ancient languages today think that the word Jesus used that is translated as 'sin' did not mean an offense against God but an error—inappropriate behavior—which is in no way the same thing. At the end of the day, the only problem with sin is that it keeps your consciousness in an inferior condition that prevents you from improving yourself."

"Meaning?"

"The more we wallow in sensory pleasures, the less we can awaken our spirituality. No one gets hurt, God has nothing to do with it, but we drag ourselves down."

Alice thought about that idea for a few seconds while Duvernet polished off the rest of his wine.

"In that case, is what Christianity calls the renunciation of sin or temptation perhaps similar to freeing ourselves from desire in Eastern religions?"

"You might say that, but Christians don't experience it that way."

Alice told herself that there could be a great difference between the present-day experience and the intention behind the original message.

"What about heaven? Lao Tzu often uses that word. What exactly does it mean in his mind?"

"In Eastern religions, heaven signifies the world of intangible, imperceptible realities. The other reality we reach by evolving, by awakening, as the Hindus call it. In English, there are different words for the *sky,* or the *heavens,* and another for the world of intangible realities: *heaven.* There is no ambiguity, while in other languages the same word can mean both things, which can lead to confusion."

"But then when Jesus tells the young man who comes to see him that if he follows his advice he will have treasure in heaven, isn't it a metaphor for the afterlife, for the paradise you can reach after death? And the famous 'kingdom of heaven' promised by Jesus, which all Christians wish to enter, isn't it also after death? Could this be the other reality Lao Tzu talks about?" Alice asked.

"Stop comparing Christianity and Taoism. They're totally unrelated!"

Duvernet was starting to get seriously annoyed. *Change the subject.*

"So tell me, what was Lao Tzu thinking when he said, 'He who dies without ceasing to be has attained immortality'?"

Duvernet let out a loud sigh. "You told me we were nearly finished."

"Nearly."

"What does that mean?"

"That's my last question."

"Finally," he grumbled.

He took another deep breath. "In most Eastern religions, the work consists of killing the former person in ourselves so we can be reborn."

"Why the hell would we do that?"

"For example, in all Vedic thought, it's the starting point—"

"What kind of thought?"

"Vedic. The Veda is a group of sacred texts that is the basis of ancient Hinduism. I was saying that in all Vedic thought, death is the starting point for imagining life. Enlightenment is not just an evolution, a progression, it is a feeling of true disruption, as if your very nature were changing. You are here, in this earthly life, a slave to your desires, with your ego and all the problems it causes, and you manage to throw yourself into the other reality of life, free of the ego, free of desires, in a fullness of being. It's as if you were dying on a certain level to be reborn on another plane."

"But that's wonderful! I finally understand Jesus's words when he said, 'For whoever wants to save their life will lose it, but whoever loses their life for me ... will save it'!"

Duvernet made a gesture of impatience. "Stop comparing Christianity with Eastern religions! They have nothing to do with each other!"

"But why wouldn't they have anything to do with each other?"

"Because most Eastern religions are non-dualistic, while Christianity *is* dualistic."

"No idea what you're talking about. You'll have to spell it out."

"Too late: you asked your last question."

"It's not a question, it's a request."

"That's the same thing."

Alice made a face. "Well, then, let's say ... that it's an order."

"You're mad."

"And you sort of like that."

He sighed and shook his head, but she could tell he was smiling slightly.

"When we look at the world around us, we see very different things."

"Certainly."

"Well, according to Eastern religions, behind that apparent diversity there is a fundamental unity. That unity might manifest itself to us in seemingly varying forms. But to realize our true nature, it is up to us to perceive, to feel the hidden unity, and to understand that man is at one with everything and everyone."

"Everything and everyone? What does that mean?"

"Every living being in the universe."

"All right, but it's still a little vague to me. I am me, you are you, we are quite distinct from each other, aren't we?"

"We are distinct, superficially, on a certain plane of reality. And yet there might be something that links us, unites us, even if I find it difficult to believe I am somehow linked to a rude young woman who's bothering the shit out of me."

"And I to believe I'm linked to a sour old man who would rather stew in his bitterness than share what he has that is precious."

His reply was simply to pour himself more wine without offering any to Alice, then to remain silent for a long time. Alice expected that he wouldn't say anything more and was thinking it was time to leave when he continued, in a much calmer tone of voice:

"You see, what is pitting us against each other right now is, in fact, our egos, that is to say, the feeling of identity we have, the feeling of self, that we are independent beings. But what we don't know is that the feeling of existing independently of others is a kind of illusion we have on a certain conscious level. When we succeed in altering that state of consciousness, we can gain access to another reality and perceive things differently."

He paused for a few seconds, calmly savoring a few sips of wine before continuing.

"Buddhists and Hindus frequently use a metaphor to illustrate the phenomenon: the wave and the ocean. If it had a brain, the wave might see itself as unique, independent, and in a certain way, that would be true: Take a wide-angle shot of the ocean

149

and choose one wave. Look at it carefully. Out of millions of waves, there is not another like it, none with the same breadth or height or shape, none with the same ripples on its surface. It is absolutely unique. And yet that wave is inseparable from the ocean. It is part of the ocean, and the ocean is part of it. In a certain way, it is the ocean."

He paused. Alice kept watching him.

He continued in a wistful tone of voice. "If I were a wave, it would probably be very pleasant, rewarding, to feel I was a unique wave, to feel I existed independently of everything else. I could be proud of being a beautiful wave. But...if I stopped clutching on to my identity as a wave, if I let it disappear, if I allowed it to die, then slowly, little by little, I would begin to feel that I was the ocean. Then I would fully become the ocean and...wow...that's something, to be the ocean..."

He fell silent and his words seemed to linger in the room.

Alice took a deep breath. She was beginning to feel the impact of these ideas within her.

"And," she said, "if we get back to people..."

He remained silent for another moment, then spoke in a slow, deep voice. "For religions that are not dualistic, whoever renounces his identity...realizes...that he is God."

His voice echoed, as if suspended in midair.

Despite the total atheist she was, Alice felt troubled by that idea.

"Eastern non-dualism," he continued, carefully pronouncing each word, "is the oneness of man and of God. Man, through the process of awakening, fully becomes God."

He turned to look at her.

"You understand that this is not comparable with Christianity, which would consider that idea blatantly blasphemous. Christianity is dualistic: God is seen as an all-powerful being to whom the believer speaks, whom he adores, implores, asks for forgiveness.

A Christian believes that devotion will free him after death. The Buddhist, Hindu, or Taoist believes that enlightenment can free him now, during his lifetime."

Duvernet poured them both more wine.

"A Christian believes in the existence of heaven and hell as real places they will go one day. Hindus know that everything is within us, everything: heaven, hell, and God. That was the great discovery revealed in the Upanishads, eight centuries before Christ."

"The Upanishads?"

"The philosophical Hindu texts."

Alice began to feel that beyond his unpleasant, sometimes aggressive attitude, Duvernet was actually a good person. She realized that she quite liked him.

"You just mentioned working toward enlightenment. What does that consist of?"

"Freeing yourself from your ego."

"So we're back to that."

"Of course! Since our normal state of consciousness doesn't allow us to realize our divine nature, we feel a certain vagueness about who we are, and that's painful. As I told you, we're afraid of not existing enough, not having enough worth. And that's why we create a reassuring false identity for ourselves: our ego. And the more we develop that false identity, the more we distance ourselves from our true nature, our divine nature. And in addition, we become unhappier: living through the ego is living in hell."

"I'm beginning to understand."

"Our ego wants us to be unique, so that it can have its own, independent existence, and to feel unique, you have to feel different. So the ego separates us from others and distances us more and more from our true nature, which tends toward the opposite: toward unity, oneness. If necessary, our ego can push some of us to opposition, conflict, division."

He coughed, then continued.

"Division. Di-vision. Double vision: my ego does not want unity, it wants duality. Some people need conflict to feel they exist!"

He smiled.

"You see," he continued, "the devil is also within us. It's an internal tendency and not some external figure."

"The devil? Why are you talking about the devil?"

"The devil, from the ancient Greek *diabolos,* is the one who divides."

He drank some wine and calmly continued.

"But if the wave is separated from the ocean, it disappears, it dies for good. It didn't know that it *was* the ocean."

Alice looked around her. The enormous vaulted wine cellar was magnificent. The stately wrought-iron wall sconces cast a yellowish light over the stone and the many oak barrels lined up in rows, creating a remarkable atmosphere. Like that of a mysterious temple.

"People need to find the connection with their divine nature," said Duvernet. "But they don't know it. Even atheists need transcendence. Have you ever wondered why people keep going to movie theaters? These days, we can download all the movies we want for very little money and watch them, chilling out on the couch. So why do people still go to the movies, with someone else's head blocking the screen, someone's knees in their back, and the sticky popcorn from the person next to them falling onto their pants?"

"Good question."

"Because a movie theater is a temple."

"What?"

"People go there to feel the same emotions, the same feelings all together at the same time, to be transported together into another world. If you look at it objectively, it's almost an experience of spiritual union."

Somewhat shaken by Duvernet's words, Alice began to feel attracted by the Eastern, non-dualistic vision.

"Several times you mentioned the states of consciousness that allow us to perceive the divine nature within us. What can help us attain the right state of consciousness?"

"According to Eastern religions, it would be meditation. Meditation allows us to focus our minds by using techniques that vary according to different schools of thought. For example, some suggest you relax while concentrating on your breathing, others on a certain part of the body, and others on an idea or poetic words. That leads to relaxation, to calming your restless Western mind, to channeling your attention and, little by little, through practice, understanding that you are not what you identify with, and to feeling within you a flow of consciousness. In that way, meditation can guide us toward a state that allows us to experience life without the ego for a few moments. That's the goal of Buddhist meditation, for example. Buddha has sometimes been called *anatma vadin,* he who teaches the non-ego. You find other forms of meditation in all Eastern religions."

"A few moments without the ego . . . and to free yourself from it once and for all?"

"Practice, practice, years of practice. Some would say for your whole life."

Alice frowned, thoughtful.

She thought back to the parishioners in Cluny as they prayed. She realized that they too were attaining an altered state of consciousness.

"Meditation sounds similar to Christian prayer."

"Except that prayer is directed to a—"

"I know. An external God."

"You're not very quick, but you end up understanding."

She smiled.

"What about you: with all your knowledge of the subject, why did you let your ego ruin your life?"

He tensed. "Why do you say that?"

"Everyone knows what happened to you. If you started to act foolishly once you were famous and your life fell apart, it must be because success went to your head, right? And that's your ego, isn't it? So why? You were knowledgeable enough to understand the risks."

He looked away, annoyed, and remained silent for a long time.

"Knowledge doesn't change things much," he said in a somber tone of voice. "There's a great difference between intellectual knowledge and internal transformation. On this point, I'm a true Westerner: here, as soon as you have understood something on an intellectual level, whether it is in the domain of psychology or spirituality, you're convinced the work is finished."

"And...you didn't practice meditation?"

"Do I look like the kind of guy who meditates two hours a day, sitting in the lotus position in front of a stack of three pebbles next to a pond of water lilies?"

# 19

THAT MONDAY MORNING, THE OFFICE LOCATED HIGH IN THE
Montparnasse Tower was flooded with a blinding light.

*All right,* thought Alice. *The Hindus believe in an internal
God, the Christians in an external one, and I don't believe in any
God, even if my ego really wants me to believe that the Hindus
are right!*

Suddenly, she was overcome with doubt.

What exactly had Jesus said about all that? She remembered he
was asked the question but had forgotten his response. If Jesus's
vision was consistent with that of the Hindus, then everything
would obviously change.

She rushed to open her *Civil Code,* full of hope. It took some
time to find the passage, despite the fact that she had read the
Gospels at least seven or eight times by now and was beginning
to know the text quite well.

She finally found it in the Gospel of Luke, chapter 17, verse

21. Answering a question a group of Pharisees had asked, he said, "The kingdom of God is already among you."

Alice closed the Bible again, very disappointed.

Too bad. In any case, she had never believed in God.

The most important thing was her unsettling discovery: Christianity, as well as Hinduism, Buddhism, and Taoism, advocated freeing yourself from your ego. She was getting closer to the exhilarating possibility that she had caught a glimpse of a universal truth.

She stretched out, leaning back in her chair.

The vision of a God that lies within was the only idea that might hold her attention. How could anyone believe in an external creative force if they had gone to school or had a higher education? Adam and Eve, the Garden of Eden, they were nice stories, but really, now we knew about the Big Bang.

She turned to her colleague, who was absorbed in his computer, as always.

"Rachid?"

He replied with a grunt, still staring at his screen.

"In your file on conference speakers, you wouldn't happen to have a physicist? Or even better, an astrophysicist?"

He sighed.

Alice waited a few seconds while he typed something.

"Jacques Laborie, PhD in astrophysics, specialist in intergalactic astronomy, a researcher at the Institute of Astrophysics in Paris. Will that do?"

"Great! How many talks has he given?"

"Let's see . . . He's given four talks to our clients."

"Good, so he wouldn't refuse to help me out for fifteen minutes! Could you arrange a brief phone call with him for me?"

"I'm not your assistant."

"Please."

"I'll see what I can do."

"You're an angel."

Alice thought no more about it and concentrated on her clients' files until lunchtime. That day, she didn't go to the company cafeteria. She was behind in her work and was only allowing herself a quick break to grab a sandwich at her desk. She put the radio on to stream through her computer. Monty Python. Perfect for a little break and to clear her mind while eating her ham sandwich.

*"I wish to register a complaint . . ."*

The shrill voice of John Cleese in the sketch with Michael Palin about the dead parrot soon made her smile.

But Alice's mind went back to the idea of letting go of the ego. Since there seemed to be a consensus about it in many religions, even if that fact wasn't well known, she was more and more motivated to try to—

*"What's wrong with it?"*

—free herself from it and re-create that extraordinary state of being she had felt for a few moments in Hermès.

It shouldn't be too difficult for her. She didn't feel she had a particularly strong ego, when she—

*"'E's dead, that's what's wrong with it!"*

—compared herself to all the self-centered people she saw constantly around her, in her company's management, at the gym she sometimes went to, and, of course, on TV, where an inflated ego seemed to be a requirement to be invited onto a program. Of course, the top prize went to the politicians: when it comes to ego, they take the cake.

*"Look, matey, I know a dead parrot when I see one . . ."*

She wanted to start right away, to take advantage of all the opportunities to practice freeing herself from her ego.

"Hi, Alice."

She looked up. It was Laure, from HR. A young blonde who was always very affected and somewhat snooty.

"Hi, Laure, how are you?"

*"He's resting."*

"Oh, you're listening to Monty Python?" she said in a slightly condescending tone.

Alice immediately picked up on the scorn in her little smile and felt ashamed. "I just turned on the radio. I don't know what's on."

"No need to make excuses," said Laure rather pointedly. "You're not obliged to listen to France Culture."

"I'm not making excuses—"

*"It's stone dead . . ."*

*"No! 'E's resting!"*

"Here, I'm leaving a file for Rachid. If you could tell him when he gets back from lunch."

She left.

Alice controlled her anger toward the colleague who looked down on her. Anger toward herself, who had failed so soon in her good intentions.

She took a deep breath and tried to calm herself.

Why was she ashamed? She was free to listen to a radio show that wasn't intellectual. What was the problem? It had nothing to do with her status or intelligence! Everyone had the right to relax, didn't they?

And besides, even if that killjoy thought she was an idiot, what difference did it actually make? It wouldn't change who she really was, so why did she feel so bad, and why had she reacted that way despite her resolution?

*"There, he moved!"*

She went over their exchange in her mind, as Toby Collins often advised, and ended up understanding: it wasn't what Laure had said—which was rather neutral in the end—that prompted Alice's ego to react but her colleague's scornful attitude. It had been obvious in her smirk, the tone of her voice, how she raised her chin slightly. And what caused Laure to act so condescending? Her ego, of course. So it was Laure's ego that had provoked her own!

*"No . . . that was you . . . "*

That was definitely it, she was sure of it now. Normally she had very little ego, didn't put on airs, and identified relatively little with her roles. But the egos of other people had the power to unleash her own in a fraction of a second, when they were trying to look good at her expense, trying to put themselves above her.

*"Testing! Testing! This is your . . . alarm call!"*

Alice then understood that she wasn't free. If other people's attitudes had the power to pull her down when she was now trying to rise to a higher spiritual level, then she wasn't free. She wanted to liberate herself from her ego, but other people's egos were keeping her tied to her own.

*"Now look, mate, I've definitely 'ad enough of this. That parrot is definitely deceased."*

She then remembered something that had happened the night before, on the way back from Cluny, in the underground parking lot of her building. She'd run into the downstairs neighbor, who was dressed up on a Sunday night as if she were going to work. Alice had just parked her dusty Renault. Wearing sneakers, she was heading for the elevator when her neighbor, wearing high heels, got out of her shiny new Mini. Alice had made an effort, with great difficulty, to be friendly, even nice. But the other woman had responded by looking Alice up and down, a superior smile on her face that clearly meant "You and I don't belong in the same world." Alice had a burning desire to let the neighbor know that their apartment had one more bedroom than hers and that with the value of that extra room, she could easily have bought two or three Minis and an entire Louboutin designer collection.

She'd known for a long time that her worth had nothing to do with her possessions, that it was just her ego talking. But it was stronger than her. Her ego was like a devil locked in a box, a box that other egos could open at will, making her suffer in the process. In the end, her ego was her greatest source of suffering.

*"The only reason it had been sitting on its perch in the first place was that it was* nailed *there."*

Alice took a deep breath. There must be a way without going so far as to meditate two hours a day.

After all, she did feel she had evolved somewhat over the past few years, without having done any specific work on her ego— whose existence she had been unaware of—simply by developing her self-esteem and confidence in herself and others. In the past, she recalled, she was much more reactive to other people's gibes. It was almost as though by learning to love herself, she had naturally lost some of her ego. That seemed paradoxical, of course. But what if an excess of ego and a lack of self-esteem were two sides of the same coin? In the end, perhaps people who strongly identified with their egos, who were bigheaded or very arrogant, were, deep down, actually insecure?

Alice sensed that continuing to develop confidence in herself, reassuring herself about her true value, would help her react less strongly to attacks and keep her own ego in check. And if other people's arrogance was caused by hidden suffering, wouldn't compassion toward them perhaps be more appropriate than reacting to them?

*"'E's passed on! This parrot is no more!"*

160

*If only I could manage to dampen my ego,* Alice thought, *to break my ties to it, free myself from it, I'd be happy, even proud to have managed it* . . . Proud? Proud? But who would be proud? *My . . . ego? Help! My ego is trying to take over my new identity as someone seeking a higher spiritual level—just like the character in the cartoon by Voutch!*

So, then . . . how could it work?

*"Well, I'd better replace it, then."*

# 20

M<small>ONDAY EVENING.</small>

"Alice, you don't look well."

"No, no, everything's all right. I'm just a little tired."

In truth, the legal conversations going on at this dinner party given by one of Paul's colleagues, who was also married to a lawyer, bored her to tears, so she was taking refuge in her thoughts. And what a ridiculous idea to have accepted an invitation on a Monday evening! Now she would be exhausted for the rest of the week.

She had a sip of champagne and took a little cake from a platter.

In the corner of the living room, one of the couple's children was watching television, stretched out on an ottoman that was bigger than him. A commercial for a men's cologne promised to transform the viewer into an irresistible superhero. Alice smiled.

The ego was such an easy lever to pull. The admen knew how to play the game. What better way to sell something than to encourage us to form a flattering image of ourselves? The simple mention of such and such product reinforced the false identity that we thought was the real us, that we thought increased our worth in others' eyes, and this made the product irresistible. The virus named "desire" had burrowed its way into our minds and would never let go until we gave in to it. And that was how money, the servant of our desires, gradually became our master, our God.

Everyone suffered from ego, their own and other people's. And today, nothing enticed us to free ourselves from it. Quite the opposite: society as a whole encouraged us to have an inflated ego, because our economic system depended on it.

The TV commercial was over and an interview with a politician came on. In the past, Alice had been fascinated by political debates, where everyone sincerely championed their view of society. Today, everyone championed their career, their campaign, their personal interests. Of course, not everyone could be Jaurès or de Gaulle, but still.

Alice caught a few bits of the exchanges. Even the journalist was less interested in how to solve society's problems than in the political game itself. Most of the questions dealt with the man's career strategies or the way he might succeed, or not, in taking power.

Alice thought that even the left-right divide was a result of and maintained by man's ego, the ego that needs to split things apart, to create opposing camps, to feel its importance to its own camp and especially against its opponent. Besides, politicians of all stripes knew this very well: to close ranks and lure voters to the polls, all they had to do was raise the specter of the other side, cry wolf, and everyone would happily fall in line without even thinking about it. The left-right divide was a powerful democratic anesthetic.

The little boy's eyes seemed glued to the television, even though he probably didn't understand much.

In another corner of the living room, the couple's teenager was engrossed in a game of air hockey against his older brother. He must have had a lot of practice because his reflexes were amazing.

Alice nibbled on her cake and watched them.

Spiritual exploration was not her specialty and she felt helpless, a feeling she resented. Her long experience in personal development had taught her something: you had to remain confident in any situation. Being confident allowed you to access your skills, which you needed to find solutions to problems. Despondency was deadly.

The teenager was skillfully using his air hockey paddle to push the puck to the opposite side and counter his brother's maneuvers. The puck was moving at incredible speed because the air pumped across the surface meant there was no friction, no resistance.

*No resistance . . .*

Alice smiled. It would be good if you could pump air across your brain to clear the ego's resistance!

She suddenly thought of Toby Collins's approach in his sessions to resistance to change. Toby always said, "It's pointless to fight it. Better to trick it." And, in fact, he had developed some techniques—sometimes funny to put into practice—to help avoid resistance.

Alice took a sip of champagne. What if she applied those techniques? Modern psychology in the service of spirituality. Why hadn't she thought of it sooner? If personal development sometimes lacked spiritual depth, spirituality severely lacked the psychological tools to help people put it to use in their lives.

She felt excited by that thought, and a few initial ideas came to mind. Cheered up, she poured herself some more champagne.

"You look better!" said the wife of Paul's colleague.

Alice smiled at her and agreed.

"It's no fun—you always win," said the older brother as he walked away. He flopped down in front of the television next to his younger brother.

"Turn the sound down a little," their mother said.

The teenager at the air hockey table caught Alice's eye. "Do you want to play?"

"Play?" she replied, laughing. "I've never played air hockey!"

"It's easy, it's like soccer."

"I've never played soccer either."

"Yeah? Well, it's no problem."

Alice hesitated a moment, then stood up. She took the paddle abandoned by the older brother and took her place across from the teenager. This was definitely more fun than listening to legal arguments.

He started by giving the puck a little push in Alice's direction, which she returned easily by giving it a little hit back. Seeing that she wasn't doing too badly, he gradually speeded things up.

Everything seemed a question of reflexes, of concentration, of getting all her faculties going so she could react in a fraction of a second. And yet Alice wasn't concentrating, not at all. Quite the opposite—she was very relaxed. Her status as an inexperienced adult meant that nothing was expected of her, she had no score to defend, no reputation to uphold. She had nothing at all to lose. So she felt unusually free and calm, responding to every movement of the puck without thinking, without asking herself tactical questions, with simply a desire to do well. Her hand and arm reacted instinctively, and Alice almost had the impression of letting them act on their own, without trying to control them through her will.

She scored a goal, which left her unmoved, and continued to let herself play without thinking about anything at all. She kept scoring goals, and the pace of the game grew faster and faster. She was in a different state, neither mentally invested nor emotionally involved in the game but not a disinterested spectator either. She was aware of what she was doing, but at the same time, she enjoyed a feeling of letting go that was unusual for her. It was as if her movements were following a kind of physical intuition, as if her hand knew what to do without obeying any orders from her brain. And it happened like clockwork, with great fluidity of movement. In a game that was now going extremely fast, she kept scoring goals with no effort at all.

The teenager declared the game was over and that Alice was the winner. She then realized he was dripping with sweat and hadn't scored a single goal.

"It's unbelievable," he said. "I've never seen anything like it. I've been practicing for four months and none of my buddies has ever beaten me. You're a pro, then, aren't you?"

"It's the first time I've played."

"No way. Hey, Arthur. Did you see?"

"Huh?" the brother replied without looking away from the television. He seemed glued to the sordid images on the news.

"Forget it," said the teenager. "Mom?"

"Yes, darling."

"Did you see your friend? She can play incredibly fast."

"I'm getting embarrassed," said Alice.

"No, really, show her. It's crazy. Look, Mom!"

He picked up his paddle. Alice took hers, flattered by his words of praise. She was glad she'd come to the party after all!

The game started up again with his mother watching.

166

Proud to be the object of so much attention, Alice concentrated. The game resumed at maximum speed. She played as best she could, but she soon realized that the magic was gone, and despite an intense game, she lost to the teenager.

"It's true that she plays well," his mother concluded.

"She played much better just before. You missed it. It was crazy!"

Alice thanked him and joined the adults.

The television in the corner of the room continued broadcasting the news of the day in front of the dazed boys.

Alice didn't want any of the champagne or salmon canapés offered to her. She felt she was in some little cloud, thinking about what had just happened.

It wasn't an air hockey match. It had nothing to do with sports, competition, or even victory and defeat. It was something else. An awareness. An understanding.

If she acted with confidence, without any egotistical motives or desire to serve her personal interests, those actions could be imbued with unbelievable, almost supernatural, power. It was as if she had been given a force over which she had no control, a power for which she was simply the medium. The wave that carried within it the strength of the ocean.

Alice took a deep breath. She caught a glimpse of everything such a discovery could mean. What it could lead to in life.

And she thought about Jesus again.

He had insisted on healing the sick out of anyone's sight and asked that no one spread the news of what he had done. Was it so that he wouldn't lose his powers by allowing his ego to claim his achievements? Or was it to set an example, to show everyone that there was a link between the renunciation of pride and the power of our actions?

She ran her fingers through her hair.

At Hermès, she had succeeded in escaping from her ego for a few moments and had experienced an unbelievable feeling of well-being. During the hockey game, she had just glimpsed the power of actions that were devoid of ego. Alice was becoming more and more convinced that the "kingdom of heaven" Jesus constantly talked about had nothing to do with a paradise after death, with the end of time, or even with the coming of a supposed holy reign. And when his disciples—who never seemed to understand anything—asked him when they might see that divine kingdom, Jesus invariably replied that it would not come as an observable event, and that it had, in fact, already begun. It did not, therefore, have anything to do with a specific event or situation set in time.

The kingdom—and she had felt this during her discussion with Raphaël Duvernet in the wine cellar of his château—must be that other reality she had perhaps experienced twice for a short time. A parallel reality to the one we all knew. One reality was temporal, the other spiritual. Day-to-day reality unfolded chronologically, every act taking place at a specific moment in time. Spiritual reality was...beyond time. It was like another dimension that was independent of this one. What's more, during the first game, she'd lost all notion of time, as well as any concerns that related to time, like scoring a goal or winning. In the second game, after her ego was in the grip of success, she recalled thinking about scoring goals and winning. Her mind anticipated the future and hoped to emerge the winner. She had returned to the temporal plane.

She smiled as she thought back to Jesus's words, which she had initially perceived as bad advice: "Tomorrow will worry about itself." She had revolted—how could someone advise others not to look ahead? She now understood that Jesus was barely concerned with the day-to-day realities of temporal life. His message had to do with another dimension into which he was inviting people.

What if this was the "eternal life" he always had been promising—eternal because it was non-temporal? She vaguely recalled the statement that had particularly made her laugh, something like "Whoever hears my word will cross over from death to life." You had to be so gullible, she'd thought at the time, to be taken in by such words, to believe that having died, you would wake up one day to have your body form again over your dried-out bones! Afterward, she had come to the idea that Jesus was perhaps using the term "death" to mean the egotistical existence. When we are controlled by our ego, we are so wide of the mark, we delude ourselves so much about who we are, that we don't live our lives, and it's as if we were dead. And according to Raphaël Duvernet, Eastern wisdom held that spiritual awakening required dying on a certain level to be reborn on another plane.

Everything seemed linked. All these hypotheses, all these interpretations converged. Eternal life was not the heaven where you'd find all the nice dead people who had behaved well during their lives. Eternal life was that other reality Alice had caught a glimpse of, a reality that was immediately accessible to the living!

"You look really strange, Alice. What on earth are you think-ing about?"

Alice started. It was Paul's colleague.

"Eternal life. What about you?"

"Ha, ha! Great way to avoid the issue." He lowered his voice to add, "You must be having sinful thoughts."

"Let's just say no one would want to hear them."

He laughed and poured her more champagne. They clinked glasses.

*Things a lot of people wouldn't be ready to hear,* she thought. *Things not easy to share.*

She sighed. It was probably best to keep it all to herself, to avoid making a fool of herself or being seen as crazy. How could anyone understand or imagine the possibility of another reality, a kind of parallel world outside of time, unless they had experienced it themselves, even if only for a few moments, as she'd had the unbelievable luck to do? Who could grasp what she had felt on those occasions?

She sensed that very few people could hear such things and believe in them. Even a few months ago, she herself wouldn't have taken it seriously.

She thought back to her CEO, whose announcement of a humiliating general freeze in salaries had unleashed her instinct to apply the Christian precept of turning the other cheek. It had been the beginning of her adventure.

She sighed again. Keeping it to herself was the wisest course. But at the same time, it was egotistical, wasn't it?

Ego-tistical.

She bit her lip. "Impossible!" she said out loud, unable to hold back.

"What?" asked the teenager.

"Nothing."

She must act in such a way that everyone might benefit from this, that everyone might see that they could stop ruining their lives because of their egos! Everyone—starting with the people she could influence quickly, easily. The people from—

"What are you doing this weekend?" another colleague asked.

"We haven't planned anything," Paul replied. "Perhaps we'll have a walk around the Marais—"

"No," said Alice. "We're going to Cluny this weekend!"

# Part III

The hour has already come for you to wake up
from your slumber...
The night is nearly over; the day is almost here.
So let us put aside the deeds of darkness
and put on the armor of light.

—Paul's Epistle to the Romans, 13:11–12

# 21

THE OLD BUTTON-TUFTED LEATHER DOOR GROANED ON ITS HINGES, then closed again with the muffled noise of a bellows. Entering the church, Alice smelled the familiar odor of damp stone lightly mixed with incense. Jeremy's voice echoed in the nave as he ended Mass. In the semidarkness, she noticed for the first time a commemorative plaque at the foot of the statue of the Virgin Mary after its restoration a few years earlier. INAUGURATED IN THE PRESENCE OF HIS GRACE FRANÇOIS D'AUBIGNIER, BISHOP OF AUTUN. His name had been carefully engraved in the bronze for posterity.

Alice silently walked up the side aisle. There were a respectable number of churchgoers, and she was happy for Jeremy. She recognized Madame de Sirdegault, sitting stiffly upright in her seat on the aisle of the first row, wearing the cross with the large ruby she always had on. Just behind her was Victor, the old winegrower who was half deaf, with Étienne, his friend who stuttered. On the other side of the central aisle sat Germaine and Cornélie, both wearing cat-eye glasses and holding a prayer book in one hand and rosary beads in the other.

The altar was bathed in natural light, and Jeremy, in his black cassock and little white collar, stood out against the dark stone walls.

He ended the service and the great organ echoed as the parishioners stood up to leave, swept along by the poignant music of Johann Sebastian Bach. Alice felt her eyes fill with tears, as they always did when she heard "Jesu, Joy of Man's Desiring." Certain artists managed to truly move you in the deepest parts of your being.

The nun Alice had nicknamed Sister IKEA walked up to her in silence and slipped a little piece of paper into her hand before walking away. Alice unfolded it: a new handwritten extract from the Gospels.

She waited patiently until the church was completely empty. The organ stopped and the last chord echoed beneath the immense vaulted ceiling, then faded away. Silence reigned once more. Alice walked over to Jeremy. He looked up when he heard her coming, greeting her with a wide smile.

"I've come back," she said, smiling at him.

"You've come back."

"I've come back to work with you."

She took a few steps around the altar, slowly, taking her time. Her footsteps echoed in the empty church.

"I think," she said, "that there are still a few things to change here."

She saw that Jeremy was listening to her with a mixture of fear and amusement.

"We need to get down to the serious matters," she said. "From now on, we're going to pass on the *true meaning* of Jesus's messages."

He raised one eyebrow.

"In short," she said, "we're going to stop all the nonsense."

He recoiled slightly. It was barely noticeable.

"You really like to provoke, don't you?" he said, sounding amused.

She gave him her best smile. Her footsteps continued echoing in the church. Everywhere on the stained-glass windows, the saints seemed to be observing her with rapt attention. At the top of one column, all three stone faces of Cluny's famous Pidou Berlu seemed to widen their eyes.

"Do you know how old people generally are when they first read Greek mythology?" she asked.

"Ten or twelve?"

"Did you know that it contains philosophical ideas of incredible depth? The kind that give you metaphysical vertigo. And yet it's rare for adults to read it. Why? Why do we leave reading mythology to kids of ten, who understand none of its deep meaning, when an intellectual of fifty could benefit from it? Because mythology is seen everywhere as a collection of fantastical stories, only good as the stuff of dreams for children. That's a shame, isn't it?"

Her last few words echoed in the nave.

"I see where you're headed," Jeremy said.

"I've become interested in the symbols and metaphors of Eastern religions. I've just read Campbell, hundreds of pages of analysis of mythologies from all over the world. And I've understood a certain number of things about the Bible that I've never heard in a Mass."

"Perhaps you didn't go to enough services."

Alice snorted with laughter. "In particular, I've realized that the external events found in the Bible describe a reality that is internal, within us. If no one tells us that, then the events in

175

question make us laugh because we find them, at best, unfounded and, at worst, grotesque."

Jeremy stiffened a little.

"If you don't tell us that Noah's flood symbolically represents the flood of impulses and emotions that destabilize us," she continued, "and you are content to talk about the ark and its nice animals who stand together calmly, it's ridiculous. Even a five-year-old understands that a lion isn't going to reach out its paw to console a seasick gazelle. And if you continue to talk about the Exodus as if Moses actually led his people from the land of slavery to the promised land, then you're going to alienate everyone who knows anything about archeology. Archeologists have dug all over the Sinai Desert and never discovered the tiniest fragment of pottery to show that six hundred thousand families lived there for nearly forty years. On the other hand, people would be a little more receptive if you explained that the text was a myth illustrating the internal path that could lead each of us from mental slavery to freedom.

"When you say that Jesus rose to heaven without explaining what the word 'heaven' means, anyone who's been to school at all will balk. If you go on and on about sin without ever explaining to us that letting ourselves indulge in too many pleasures will compromise our chance to awaken ourselves to something else more beautiful, then you will be seen as castrating killjoys. And that is definitely true of all Jesus's parables: if you don't give us the keys to decode them and understand the useful messages they hold, then everyone will laugh at them—me first of all—and the churches will be empty."

Jeremy sighed. "I think you're being a bit harsh."

"The moment comes when you have to gauge the consequences of your actions."

"You seem very sure of yourself when it comes to the consequences of our actions, in any case."

She smiled. "Listen: a recent survey showed that 34 percent of Frenchmen believe in the devil as a real being. There's the consequence of your actions. And 59 percent of Americans. You've succeeded even more over there."

Silence fell once more in the church.

"Aren't you exaggerating a little?" he timidly suggested.

Alice smiled again. "Look at your busybodies."

"Who?"

"Germaine and Cornélie! They know their prayer book by heart. Do you think they seem enlightened?"

Alice guessed he was suppressing a smile.

Then he shook his head in a disapproving way. "Jesus said: 'Why do you look at the speck of sawdust in your brother's eye and pay no attention to the plank in your own eye?'"

"Okay, point taken," Alice replied. "But *I* haven't spent sixty years assiduously attending a place of worship."

He looked rather abashed and sighed.

"This is the twenty-first century, Jeremy! Wake up! Wake up so you can hope to wake us up."

He remained silent for a long time before speaking. "So you want me to explain the metaphors, is that it?"

"Yes."

"The problem is that not everyone is mature enough to receive the messages. That's why Jesus spoke in parables when he spoke to the crowds, while he didn't hesitate to explain everything to his apostles, who were close to him."

Jeremy seemed to waver. Alice felt she had shaken his conviction but he was still resisting.

"You mentioned Eastern religions," he said. "Eastern spiritual masters abide by the principle that the disciple comes to them and asks questions. They themselves recommend never telling people things they aren't ready to hear."

"I'm sure that a lot of people *are* ready."

He shook his head, deep in thought. "Jesus advised great prudence in this area."

"If you're too prudent, you don't do anything."

"He even said: 'Give not that which is holy to the dogs, neither cast you your pearls before swine, lest they trample them under their feet, and turn again and rend you.'"

"Your parishioners would appreciate that comparison."

Jeremy burst out laughing. "Don't make me say something I don't mean, or believe!" He shook his head before adding, "You are truly incorrigible! And you can't see where all of this risks leading us."

"It's not my fault. I have a plank in my eye."

He sighed deeply. "Fine . . . So you want me to explain the parables. What else? Because I'm assuming it doesn't end there."

She smiled. "No one can hide anything from you."

"Well?"

"There's another problem with the church, in my opinion, and that's that they ask you to believe without proof, without experience. Hinduism calls for people to experience things."

"So what are you proposing?"

"I'm proposing spiritual exercises inspired by personal development that will allow those who wish to free themselves of their ego, their mental state, to do so, so they can experience the other reality as much as possible, the 'other side,' as Jesus called it."

"Alice, with all the goodwill in the world, we are still in church. It's a place of worship! We can't start doing *exercises*. We're not with Toby Collins! It's necessary to respect the traditions of the church."

"Traditions? But Jesus was the fiercest opponent of traditions!

He healed the sick on the Sabbath even though it was strictly forbidden by tradition. He ate whatever he wanted, even though tradition imposed strict dietary laws."

"Alice, I am required to follow the liturgical codes. Do you understand that?"

"Must I remind you of Isaiah's words that Jesus himself repeated at the time? 'These people honor me with their lips, but their hearts are far from me. They worship me in vain; their teachings are merely human rules.' As for places of worship, we shouldn't sanctify them more than necessary. Besides, Jesus rarely went to them, except to argue with the merchants."

Jeremy shook his head and smiled. But Alice could tell she was gaining ground.

"Let's not confuse the end and the means," she said. "Your traditions are speeches and rituals invented in a distant past as the best way of getting messages across to people. Times have changed, people have evolved, yet your traditions remain immutable? Two thousand years ago science was in a primitive state, no one understood the universe, people were full of stupid fears, superstitions, and beliefs. Perhaps all that was necessary was to add new beliefs for them to become followers, since human beings need to have meaning. Not today. People are intelligent and sophisticated. No one can believe in such ridiculousness. They need to understand. People need to have things explained, and experience them."

Jeremy did not reply.

"Take Hinduism," she said. "Two thousand eight hundred years ago, the masters of the Upanishads broke with Vedic rituals to get closer to the deep meaning of the messages of the Veda. It's time to do the same thing today in Christianity, rather than clinging on—in the name of so-called tradition—to words that have lost all meaning to the great majority of people."

Jeremy frowned.

"What do you suggest," she said, "as a method to help your flock rid themselves of their ego? Flagellation? Hair shirts?"

"The good thing about you is that you never exaggerate."

Alice laughed, then said, "Take guilt. For centuries, guilt has ruined the lives of Christians without bringing them anything. What if we tried something else?"

Jeremy remained silent, looking thoughtful.

"There are more than two billion Christians in the world," Alice continued. "How many of them have managed to see the light? How many were able to attain the other reality that is opened up when the ego disappears? You've been working at it for two thousand years! Jesus must be turning over in his grave!"

He raised his eyes slowly to look at her.

"He's no longer in his grave, Alice."

# 22

"HE'S NOT HERE."

"Keep trying! Maybe he went to the bathroom."

The secretary did not reply, and Alice once again heard the phone ringing and ringing. It had been at least two weeks since she made a phone appointment with Jacques Laborie, the famous astrophysicist. He couldn't stand her up.

The phone kept on ringing and finally someone answered.

"Monsieur Laborie?"

"Yes."

Alice felt relieved. "We have a call scheduled. I'm Al—"

"Yes, we *had* a call scheduled at two and now I barely have any time to spare."

"At two? I'd written down two thirty. I'm so sorry."

"I have very little time, so we'll have to postpone our conversation, unless ten minutes will be enough to answer your question. It all depends on how complex it is."

"It's not at all complicated: I just want to understand how the world got created."

She heard him laughing.

"Is that all?"

"The short version would be fine. And simple, if possible: my knowledge of physics is less than rudimentary."

"All right."

A brief silence.

"Everything started with the void," he said, "an extremely small and dense void, full of energy, in which there was a gigantic explosion, the origin of the universe."

"The Big Bang, I assume."

"That's right. It happened about 14 billion years ago. There was so much energy released that the universe expanded in every direction. Since then, it has continued to expand, so much so that the galaxies are getting farther and farther away from each other. An enormous quantity of particles was born out of the chaos of the Big Bang, and they gathered together to form complex systems. The only chemical elements the Big Bang gave off were helium and hydrogen, very simple elements that cooled and contracted under their own weight. Atoms then joined together to form molecules. Matter became concentrated and fragmented. Under extreme pressure, the overheated gas combusted. That was the power of thermonuclear fusion. The first stars were born."

"Did life begin at that moment?"

"Life in the biological sense of the term happened much later. First, 4.5 billion years ago, there was the creation of our sun, a star surrounded by eight planets, one of which was Earth. Life began here 3.8 billion years ago, and the ancestors of man, only a few million years ago."

"What allowed life to begin?"

"The thermonuclear fusion at the heart of the first stars synthesized heavy chemical elements. When these stars—each a kind of enormous sun—exploded, they scattered those chemical elements, which came from deep within them, throughout space. On planet Earth, those fragments of stars came together to form life. The smallest atom in our bodies is nothing more than stardust, to use the term so dear to Hubert Reeves."

*Stardust.*

Alice thought back to the Eastern religions' idea of a fundamental unity, which Raphaël Duvernet had spoken about. His words echoed once more in her mind: "But to realize our true nature, it is up to us to perceive, to feel the hidden unity, and to understand that man is at one with everything and everyone."

She said, "I have another question that is gnawing at me."

"I'm very sorry, but I don't have any more time. Let's set up another time to talk if you'd like. I'll be gone for three weeks at the observatory in Middlebury, Vermont, so I suggest we speak when I return. What about Wednesday, August 10, at two?"

"Perfect!"

"Remember: two o'clock, right?"

Alice thanked him and hung up. She felt reassured in her understanding of things. Even though she had no explanation for the parallel universe she had caught a glimpse of, physics had a good explanation of the creation of the material world. No God was necessary for the chemical reactions of the universe!

*       *       *

It was warm that afternoon in her father's garden. Sitting comfortably around the wrought-iron table, in the shade of the old walnut tree, Alice and Jeremy were eating orange cake. The hot teapot gave off the scent of rose and jasmine.

As her 5 percent increase in salary wasn't enough to pay for a family trip to Australia, Alice had decided to spend the summer vacation in Cluny. Less exotic, of course, but at least there were no poisonous spiders or crocodiles in the rivers! Paul had protested, so she had taken advantage of his weak spot: "Sign up for a drawing class for the whole summer with J. P. Gillot, on the Rue Mercière. He's so gifted that he could transform a house painter into a Rembrandt." Paul let himself be convinced.

She took a bite of cake while listening to Jeremy read out loud. Mmmm . . . delicious.

> *This may seem paradoxical, but to free yourself from your ego, it is advised that you begin by developing your ego, but in a healthy way. In fact, if your ego is damaged, for example because some personal event stopped you from building your self-esteem, the suffering that resulted will unconsciously drive you to overcompensate for that damage through disproportionately egotistical attitudes. Your ego will seek to regain the upper hand, to exist toward and against everything, and will develop in an unbalanced way. You then risk losing yourself in the abyss of false identities, which your ego will cling to.*

"I can't use that as a sermon," said Jeremy. "It's totally devoid of doctrine. I'm a priest, not a professor!"

"Keep going. We'll discuss it afterward!"

He sighed, visibly annoyed, but continued reading.

> *Fighting against your ego is not a solution either. That would only cause it to get stronger, while resulting in a destabilizing sense of guilt and internal conflict. Moreover, Jesus said, "If a kingdom is divided against itself, that kingdom cannot stand."*

"That point is very important," she said. "You could make an analogy with a diet: fighting against your desire for chocolate doesn't work."

"As long as we don't illustrate with Jesus's words taken out of context, like 'Blessed are you who hunger now, for you will be satisfied.'"

Alice burst out laughing. She took another bite of orange cake as he continued:

> *This is why, for the past several months in this church, we have learned to love ourselves. Once our self-esteem is found, it is easier to free ourselves from the grip of the ego. It will then be a matter of letting go of our false identities, the roles that we play, to become again one with ourselves, and to discover the value of our existence independent of what we do or what we have. In this way, we can learn not to forget ourselves but to go beyond our own being and, without seeking any personal benefit, discover the power and strength of our actions.*

"Good," said Alice. "What do you think?"

He didn't reply, which was a rather good sign.

"You can adapt it by adding some Catholic spices if you like," she added.

Jeremy remained silent, deep in thought.

She took a sip of the hot tea.

"What are you thinking about?" she asked.

"The Curé of Ars."

"Who's that?"

"A nineteenth-century clergyman."

"Oh. Why are you thinking about him?"

He took a moment before replying. "I often think about him. He's a little like a role model to me. His superiors found his sermons weak in doctrine, and his bishop did everything he could to prevent their publication. And yet everyone recognized that he contributed to changing the lives of his parishioners. Some people even consider him a saint."

Alice stopped herself from shouting "Victory!" but she knew she had won.

A little later, when she walked Jeremy to the square in front of the church, she felt confident. He would know how to pass on these messages, which were so useful to people.

She watched him walk away, then disappear into the rectory.

"Excuse me, miss?"

She turned around.

A couple in their thirties was looking at her shyly. They were holding hands, like children, which was rather touching.

"Hello," she said, smiling.

The married couple looked at each other, as if each one expected the other to speak. They both had very sweet faces. The woman's chestnut-brown hair was pulled back into an untidy ponytail. In the end, she was the one who spoke.

"Do ya know where we can find Father Jeremy?"

"You've just missed him. He's gone, and I know he's not available right now."

They looked very disappointed.

"He'll be saying Mass tonight," she added. "You could definitely speak to him afterward."

"Tonight won't be possible—not tonight."

"We're not from the parish," the man added. "We come from Charolles, and it's far."

"My husband is a night watchman. He works tonight, so we can't stay."

Alice sensed they were worried, and a little embarrassed at the same time, as if they were in a very difficult situation.

"Do you want me to get a message to him?"

They looked at each other again.

"Actually," said the woman, "we wanted him to baptize our baby."

"Do you know Father Jeremy?"

"No, we'll have to talk to him," said the man. "We'll come back."

Alice watched them walk away, hand in hand. Why on earth would you have a child baptized in Cluny when you lived in Charolles, forty kilometers away?

She went back to her father's house, thinking about Jeremy.

He feared seeing his flock disappear. She was convinced they would stay, and even that their numbers would grow. But it was risky, of course, and *she* didn't have anything to lose. Even if she were wrong and misguided, she wouldn't suffer any consequences. For Jeremy, on the other hand, a great deal was at stake: he had chosen to dedicate his life to the church, and now his superiors viewed him badly because of her. But perhaps they were turning a blind eye because of his popularity. If his flock turned away from him, that would be the end of his ministry.

She was aware of all that, and yet something was driving her to lead Jeremy down this path. She felt it like a mysterious calling.

# 23

"WHO ARE YOU?" THE WOMAN ASKED IN A SOFT, DEEP VOICE.

She was a brunette in her forties, one of the new parishioners. She had turned her straw-backed chair to face her neighbor, in the last row of the church.

"I am...someone who works hard," replied the young man in his thirties.

"You're someone who works hard, and perhaps sometimes you are also lazy," she said in a kindly tone of voice. "And it's nice to know you can be both at the same time."

The man slowly agreed, taking in those unusual words at his own pace.

"Who are you?" the woman asked again.

"I am...someone whose work is acknowledged," he said.

"You are someone whose work is acknowledged, and perhaps sometimes you are also someone people ignore. And it's nice to know you can be both at the same time."

Alice took a few steps down the side aisle and listened to another two people from a distance. She was nervous, for the presentation of this rather psychological exercise had received a very cold welcome from the churchgoers. Jeremy had had to use a great deal of finesse and persuasion to explain and justify it.

Alice walked back up the aisle in silence. In the church, everyone finally seemed to be participating in the game, even if some of the older ones were gritting their teeth. The churchgoers had been split into pairs, and each seemed to be scrupulously following the instructions for the exercise.

Jeremy had remained near the altar. He was attentively, and nervously, scrutinizing the group.

Alice had thought up this drill, loosely based on an exercise used by the great American psychologist Stephen Gilligan. There were three goals: to prevent identifying ourselves with our roles or attributes, to accept the other side of the coin that is often present in us but repressed, and, finally, to unite apparently disparate elements in us while letting go of our image or our need for perfection. Accepting one's limitations and yielding to a certain sense of vulnerability also helped make the shift toward an awareness of the present moment and a feeling of unified harmony.

Jeremy had been cautious and taken his time when presenting the exercise to the parishioners. He had introduced it by quoting Jesus: "I do not pray for these alone, but also for those who will believe in Me through their word, that they all may be one … that they also may be one in Us … that they may be made perfect in one."

Viewed from outside, the exercise seemed very strange, but experiencing it for themselves left no one indifferent, and each person appeared to find a new kind of internal peace. Alice smiled at the thought that a visitor wandering into the church would undoubtedly have the impression that they had stumbled upon some odd sect.

She discreetly walked over to two women.

"Who are you?" the first woman asked.

Her partner, a woman in her fifties, looked very sad and remained silent for a long time before responding in a soft voice. "I am a woman alone."

"You are a woman alone, and perhaps sometimes you are also a woman who is connected to others. And it's nice to know you can be both at the same time."

She waited for a few seconds before continuing.

"Who are you?"

"I am . . . misunderstood."

Her partner took a deep breath.

"You are misunderstood, and perhaps sometimes you are also . . . understood. And it's nice to know you can be both at the same time."

Alice started when she felt a hand on her shoulder, and she turned around quickly. It was Sister IKEA, who handed her a tiny bit of folded paper. Alice opened it up. As usual, it was an extract from the Gospels.

She thanked her with a smile and took a few steps, automatically putting the note into her bag, until she was within hearing distance of Étienne and Victor talking.

"What?"

"Wh-who are you?" Étienne stammered.

"What? I don't understand this exercise at all!"

"Just t-tell me wh-who you are!" said Étienne, doing his best to talk louder.

"Who I am, who I am . . . I am . . . someone who's intelligent, that's for sure," replied Victor confidently.

"Y-you are s-someone who's in-intelligent, and you are per-perhaps also some-times someone who is si-si-silly."

"What?"

"Y-you . . . are si-silly."

"Eh?"

"Y-you . . . are si-silly," said Étienne, exhausted.

"Talk louder!"

"You . . . you're an ass!" he shouted.

Victor was so shocked that he slapped Étienne, who burst out laughing.

"And it's ni-nice . . ."

Just in front of them, a man of twenty-five or thirty wearing blue glasses was facing Madame de Sirdegault, who was obviously exasperated by the exercise.

Jeremy walked quietly over to them.

"Who are you?" the man asked.

"Everyone knows who I am!"

"Yes, but for the exercise, you have to answer."

She sighed loudly. "I hold the title of baroness, as you know very well, young man."

"You may have that title but who are you?"

"Now, really! I have a reputation everyone knows."

"Yes, I understand what you have, but who are you?"

"I keep telling you! My name is sufficiently well known in this area. The Sirdegault family had a plaque bearing its name on a bench in this church before you were even born, my poor man!"

"I'm not asking what you have but who you are."

"This is all ridiculous! I have faith, I do, I am a believer, so why are you annoying me?"

"You also have faith, but you actually have many things."

Madame de Sirdegault was seething.

191

"This is driving me crazy. You're making my blood boil!" she shouted.

Just behind her, Victor, who had finally understood the exercise and thought those words were meant for him, replied: "And this is also making you feel well and good about yourself, and that's nice."

"Amen," murmured Jeremy, with a little smile.

Alice's liturgical program, if the name could be applied to this cocktail of personal development and spiritual awakening, aimed at transmitting what she had understood about Jesus's messages, lasted several weeks. It alternated between explanatory sermons, practical exercises, and prayers meant to guide the parishioners to experience the *other side,* the other reality, which was also the goal of Buddhist meditation, according to Duvernet.

"We can truly feel the voice of another world within us," said the philosopher Ernest Renan, "but we don't know what that world is." Alice was convinced that experiencing it was the best way to understand it.

She had pushed, in vain, to rename a certain number of prayers "meditations," in order to touch a greater number of people, people who might be put off by the word "prayer." Jeremy had refused.

"You're going too far. We're still in a church, after all!"

"Admit that it's the same thing."

"Not at all—a prayer is speaking to God."

Alice made a face. "Must I remind you that Jesus said, 'Not everyone who says to me, "Lord, Lord," will enter the kingdom of heaven'?"

But she hadn't insisted.

The churchgoers had ended up getting used to the new liturgy and even reaping benefits from it. By word of mouth, the church continued to fill up more and more each week.

But what attracted the most people remained confession, something else Alice had revisited. She had invented the concept of "paradoxical penitence," whose aim was to free a person from their ego by playing down their egotistical tendencies and learning to laugh at them. Laughing at oneself would allow a person to take a step back from events, and had health benefits as well. The idea was also to provoke a true awareness of a person's tendencies, to see what was naturally ridiculous about them, so the ego would find it difficult to feed on them. The ego is to the unconscious what toothpaste is to the tube: once it's come out, just try and put it back inside.

The two gossips, Germaine and Cornélie, were certain that Alice was partly responsible for the changes in their parish's traditions. They secretly shot her acrimonious looks and turned away when she passed close by. Alice was equally mistrustful of them and watched them out of the corner of her eye.

One Sunday morning, in front of the church, she had overheard bits of their conversation with Madame de Sirdegault.

"We have to do something," Germaine had said.

"It can't go on like this any longer," Cornélie had added.

"You have a lot of influence, you could actually take steps!"

"I already have," Madame de Sirdegault replied haughtily.

The two busybodies watched the baroness walk away, then went over to Étienne to continue their efforts at sabotage.

★   ★   ★

Jeremy twisted around to try and stretch out his legs. A victim of his own success, he had been locked in the narrow confessional for more than two hours and was beginning to get cramps.

"Someone contradicted me, Father," said a woman's voice. "One of my husband's friends. We were having a drink outside at a café. He contradicted me, and I realized he was trying to point out that I was wrong. I felt...annoyed, almost...a little humiliated. Rejected. Perhaps it was the sin of pride on my part."

"Was that the first time it happened to you?"

"No, in fact it happens regularly, and not only with him. I feel bad when someone openly disagrees with me. I'd so like to be able to have a quick comeback, but I can't."

Jeremy thought for a few seconds.

"The next time you find yourself in that situation, tell yourself, 'I am my opinions.'"

"I am my opinions?"

"Right. 'I exist essentially through my opinions, my ideas, my words.'"

"I don't understand."

"Tell yourself, 'My personal worth is limited to the value of my words. If they are wrong or perceived as wrong, it's because I'm worthless.'"

Silence.

"Do you really think so, Father?"

"Tell yourself, 'By disagreeing with me, that man is picking on me.'"

"Maybe he really is."

"Then take it upon yourself to prove that you're right. Don't even wait for the other person to finish his thought. As soon as you realize he's disagreeing, interrupt him and affirm your point of view, without allowing him to speak. If he replies, cut him off and repeat what you said. You must have the last word. When it's done, tell yourself, 'I've preserved my worth. Now I'll be respected.' And if ever, when you hear the first objection from the other person, you realize that he's right and that you made a mistake, don't admit it. Never change your opinion; on the contrary, stick to your original idea: affirm it, hammer it home, impose it. Repeat this experience a dozen times."

"But...I...couldn't do such a thing."

"If you can't manage it, look to politicians as an example. They're very gifted at it."

"I'm...not sure that's a good idea."

Even though he was safely out of sight behind his wooden screen, Jeremy stopped himself from smiling, for fear that his voice might betray his amusement.

"Are you disagreeing with me?"

"Well...let's say that I don't entirely agree."

He made his voice sound very hurt. "No, you are, you are disagreeing with me."

"I'm very sorry, but...I'm having trouble agreeing."

He allowed silence to fall, then took on a particularly wounded, depressed tone of voice. "You're rejecting your priest, aren't you, my daughter?"

"But no, not at all!" she hurriedly said to justify herself.

"You no longer respect me at all."

"Of course I do!"

"You no longer respect me. I can see that."

"That has nothing to do with it!"

Silence.

Then she burst out laughing. She was laughing so hard it echoed throughout the nave.

Jeremy peeked out from behind the curtain and saw Germaine and Cornélie in the central aisle, looking indignant.

"Thank you, Father," said the woman's voice. "I think I'll experience controversy in a different way from now on."

"So be it."

A minute later, after having stretched out his legs as best he could, Jeremy heard a man's voice.

"Hello, Father. The other day, I took my son to his friend's house. A birthday party. I spoke with the father a bit, you know, small talk, very relaxed. At the time, I thought we would get along and might see each other again. But when I heard he was plant manager of a factory, that made me feel strange. It's stupid, but I felt...a little ashamed not to be on the same level as him. Normally, I'm proud of my career. I'm in industrial sales. Before, I was a technician, I worked hard to get promoted, and I'm proud of that. But then, when he told me his job, I didn't feel as good as him, as if I were...inferior. I thought I didn't want to see him again. Or maybe wait until later, after I'd managed to get a better job."

Jeremy took a deep breath. "Next time, in the same situation, tell yourself that that man is more important than you."

"You're being a bit harsh."

"To deserve his friendship, you must raise your social status."

"Well, that's true."

"After that, stop seeing your family and friends, and spend your evenings and weekends working more, in order to get a promotion. Once you get it, don't rest on your laurels. To stay motivated to work more, continue to feel you are less worthy when in the presence of anyone who has a higher social status than yours. You'll see. It's very effective."

"All right."

"Keep climbing the ladder at work. And remember to feel bad whenever there's someone above you."

This time there was a silence. When the man started talking again, the enthusiasm was gone from his voice. "But...there will always be someone above me!"

"That's the reason you have to always dedicate yourself body and soul to climbing the social ladder. You will not truly exist until the day when you are in the top position."

When the man did not reply, Jeremy added, "I propose that you think about all that for a while." But he knew that the seed of the idea was already planted.

It was starting to get hot. The confessional was fine in winter, but in summer, it soon turned into an oven.

The next person to confess was another man. His typically masculine problem made Jeremy smile: he got annoyed, really steamed up, every time someone pulled away from a red light faster than him.

"All right," Jeremy said to him, "the next time that happens, tell yourself: 'I no longer exist, I no longer have any value, I'm worthless, because my personal value depends on how fast my car can accelerate. I should be ashamed to have failed, my family in the car should be ashamed for me, and all the passersby who saw what happened are looking at me as if I am depraved, a subhuman who ruined his life.'"

The man started to laugh. Jeremy continued.

"Make yourself take off first at the next light, and if you succeed, congratulate yourself: 'That's right, now I'm really someone. Everyone will know my worth, everyone will admire me. My life is a success.' Repeat this a dozen times, no matter what happens."

The man left the confessional laughing.

"When a woman is more beautiful than me, I'm unhappy," the next woman confessed. "Yesterday, someone called the secretary of the Sales department beautiful in front of me and I felt bad."

"You're right to feel bad, because that woman is also more intelligent than you."

Silence.

"What—"

"She's also in better shape than you."

"But—"

"She's also more sophisticated than you."

"But...how do you know? I—"

"She is more spiritual than you."

"But—"

"She is more fulfilled in her work than you."

"But that's not true!"

Her voice echoed through the church.

Jeremy let silence fall again.

"This session is over," he whispered.

# 24

Madame de Sirdegault got out of her car. She had just parked in the small private parking lot of the Chalon Bridge Club when she saw Madame Fontaine, another member of the club, shutting her car door at the very same moment. A brunette with short hair, her chubbiness skillfully hidden beneath her elegant clothing, she was a woman whose sympathy was reserved for certain well-chosen people. People who did not include Madame de Sirdegault.

"How are you?" asked Madame Fontaine with an unusually cheerful smile.

Madame de Sirdegault quickly understood the reason for her unusual cheerfulness: she had the newest Louis Vuitton bag over her shoulder, the one that all the magazines were advertising, the one that every woman longed for.

She forced herself to greet Madame Fontaine with a slight nod of the head, then turned her back to put her key into her car's manual lock. It was old, of course, but at least it was a Jaguar!

However, the other woman, who normally kept her distance, suddenly came closer.

"You're early today!" she called out.

It was obvious that she didn't give a damn. It was just an excuse to show off. Madame Fontaine continued to stay with her, almost waving the bag in front of her face.

Madame de Sirdegault walked briskly toward the door of the club. She felt a pain in her stomach, as if some sadist were slowly wrenching her insides.

"This sunshine is so nice," the other woman continued. "I must say, it took long enough this year!"

*A hen,* thought Madame de Sirdegault. *She sounds like a cackling hen.*

That evening, alone in the semidarkness of the stately private residence in Cluny that her ex-husband had conceded as part of the divorce, she thought back to that annoying encounter. It was the same every time. Whenever someone bragged about possessions that she didn't have, she grew angry, with even a touch of hatred. Angry to be insulted that way, angry above all not to be able to compete since her divorce, as she no longer had the means. This spoiled her day, sometimes the evening as well, and whenever she chanced upon the guilty parties again, the resentment surged up in her like smoldering embers that catch fire in the hearth when everyone thought the flames had gone out.

She had confessed these demons to Father Jeremy's predecessor. She still remembered his reply. Quoting Jesus, he had said: "For where your treasure is, there your heart will be also." That was very beautiful, it had moved her, of course, and she had often thought back to it. But there was just one thing: it didn't change her resentment, her automatic emotional responses, her uncontrollable thoughts in the presence of a hen like Madame Fontaine.

She thought of Father Jeremy. She didn't have the courage to go and see him. She didn't approve of his methods, which didn't respect tradition, and she had even alerted the bishop on more than one occasion.

She opened the cabinet, took out a bottle of brandy, and poured a few drops into a small liqueur glass.

Holding the glass, she walked over to the tall, small-paned windows. The ancient herringbone parquet floor creaked beneath her feet. The old windows, whose surface was somewhat rippled, slightly distorted the scene outside. Above the rooftops of the medieval houses, the church's bell tower seemed to lean gently toward her.

Most of the parishioners appreciated Father Jeremy's methods—especially the newcomers, mainly young people. She sighed. Perhaps she was already too set in her ways to enjoy anything new.

She took a sip of the brandy, savoring the delicate hints of almond. It was Jacoulot. She smiled, thinking she had been drinking the same brand for at least thirty years.

The bell tower seemed to lean a little more toward her. The parishioners who went to confession with Father Jeremy seemed delighted. The conversations in front of the church were often about what had been discussed during confession. Some people laughed about it, others mentioned the benefits they had drawn from it. It was obviously very tempting.

Even Germaine and Cornélie seemed intrigued, despite everything. Of course, they continued to vehemently denounce the priest's methods in confession, which they had heard of second-hand, but didn't such passionate protestation hide some repressed desire?

She took another sip of brandy and suddenly wondered if that thought might not apply to herself. The idea upset her, and that evening, she went to bed confused.

When she woke up the next morning, she made up her mind. She dressed and put on her makeup with great care, as she did every day, then put on her jewelry. She was aware of the ridiculous nature of her situation: to get all dressed up to go to confess her attachment to material things. But people don't change, and besides, it was unthinkable to her to set a foot outside without looking her best, retaining her status, and preserving her reputation as the most elegant woman in Cluny.

When she was ready, she went to the church. Several people were waiting in the semidarkness of the side aisle, and she had to stand in the small line, which displeased her greatly. The perfume of the woman in front of her hung in the air. Cheap perfume.

She was certain that Father Jeremy would recognize her voice, and it cost her a lot to admit her shameful acts this way.

She forced herself to do it with dignity.

When she had finished, silence fell once more, and she waited, stoically, for the priest to deliver her penance.

"You will gather together your most beautiful clothes..."

"Very well."

"And put them all on."

She frowned. "Put them all on?"

"Yes."

"Father, I think you are going to have to explain what you mean."

"It's very simple: you will put all your clothes on, in layers."

"In layers?"

"Exactly."

"I don't understand."

"I think you do."

How could something so ridiculous be demanded as penance?

She could feel her anger rising and forced herself to take deep breaths to control herself. Her voice mustn't betray her annoyance.

"Let's be reasonable: that's unimaginable."

What had come over her to make her go to confession with this young whippersnapper?

"Then you will get all your jewelry together..."

"My jewelry?"

"And wear it all together."

"Wear all my jewelry?"

"Yes."

"All of it together?"

"Correct."

Ridiculous.

She could feel her tension climbing several more notches.

"Then," he continued, "you will get all your makeup."

"My makeup."

She was controlling her anger to such an extent that her lips were trembling and her voice was barely audible.

"You will put on several layers of foundation..."

"Foundation."

"Several layers of eye shadow..."

"Eye shadow."

She could scarcely hear her own voice.

Why was a sadistic pervert allowed to officiate in Cluny? She felt like a pressure cooker whose lid was tightly screwed down.

"Three layers of mascara..."

"Mascara."

What on earth was the bishop thinking?

"Four layers of lipstick..."

"But that is all pointless!" she finally exploded. "Imagine me dressed up like that! I'd suffocate! If I had all that on, no one would even be able to see me!"

Her voice echoed in the church, and in her mind.

The priest said nothing.

Absolutely nothing.

She left the confessional upset, confused. She went home and stayed in for the rest of the day. The last words she had said kept going around and around in her mind, haunting her.

*I'd suffocate! If I had all that on, no one would even be able to see me!*

That evening, calm again, holding a glass of brandy, the almost-empty bottle close by, she thought about the meaning of the words that had come out of her mouth in that moment of anger.

# 25

Théo's happy face was a pleasure to see. Sitting nicely in his turquoise patio chair, his elbows resting on the little fuchsia-colored metal table, he was enjoying an enormous scoop of peach ice cream that spilled over the edges of his cone.

Alice loved going to Louise's, the ice cream parlor just beneath the ancient door of the abbey. From the makeshift terrace on the rough, badly joined old cobblestones, amid the golden stone that pleasantly reflected the sun's warmth, there was a wonderful view of the sunlit ruins below.

Alice was calmly drinking her coffee when she noticed, in the distance, the couple from Charolles who had wanted to see Jeremy one Saturday. They recognized her and came over.

"This is a bit of luck," said the woman. "We were hoping we'd run into you."

"Me?"

"Father Jeremy's never 'round when we come, and, well, we've got a rather strange request. We heard if we went through you, we'd have a better chance of convincin' him."

"Who told you that?"

"A woman outside the church."

"Okay . . . But you don't need any support if you're asking for a baptism, you know."

The woman, visibly uneasy, looked at her husband for help.

"Actually, the priest in Charolles refused to baptize our child, so we asked the ones in the villages nearby."

"He refused? Why on earth would he refuse?"

The woman again looked to her husband for help, in vain.

"Well, when we baptized the older one, we agreed to send him to catechism classes. And . . . we didn't. It's not our fault—he doesn't want to go. We talked to him about it, tried to encourage him. He doesn't want to. We can't force him. But the priest said that under the circumstances, he wouldn't baptize the baby."

Alice wondered what problem the priest had with baptizing the second child. She must be missing something.

"And then," the woman continued, "the priests from the other parishes also refused, because everyone knew, you see? We're in a bind."

Alice sighed. "And you really want him to be baptized?"

They opened their eyes wide.

"Of course," said the woman. "It's absolutely necessary!"

"It would be terrible if he wasn't," her husband added.

Alice couldn't understand what would be so terrible about it, but he sounded so sincere that she was moved.

"I'll talk to Father Jeremy," she finally said.

"Oh, thank you!"

She thought they were both about to fall on their knees in front of her.

"I'm sure he'll agree," she added to reassure them.

206

"Really?"

"I think so."

"Oh, thank you! Thank you!"

"You're welcome."

"You promise, right?"

Alice was touched by the sight of them, holding hands. They seemed to be pleading. She agreed.

★  ★  ★

The bishop nervously twisted his amethyst ring while walking past the tall windows in his episcopal office. Outside, clouds were gathering in the sky. The wind was up, an omen of an impending storm. The air already carried the scent of it.

"You have been very patient until now, Your Grace," said the curate.

He was standing, as straight as always. He had gray hair and features marked by intransigence, despite his youth.

The bishop did not reply. He had always approved of some freedom in the parishes, but it was true that Father Jeremy was going a bit too far.

"He doesn't listen to us," the curate insisted, pinching his lips together.

Outside, the first drops of rain were falling. The swallows flew swiftly and close to the ground in an impromptu ballet.

The bishop thought back to the reports he had heard. Everyone agreed. Father Jeremy was losing his way.

"We must persevere," said the bishop. "Let's try to reason with him."

"A waste of time. He pays no attention whatsoever to our advice."

The rain was falling hard now. The little foals from the neighboring field set off at a gallop.

"Jesus tells us that we must find the lost sheep," said the bishop.

"This lost sheep doesn't want to come back into the fold, Your Grace."

The bishop sighed. By all accounts, his curate was right.

"We are risking the image of our entire diocese," the curate continued.

The truth was not so simple. There was very little chance that Father Jeremy's deviations would reach the Holy See. The growing number of his congregation, on the other hand, could only serve the church. The pope appreciated those bishops capable of bringing the flock back to the church.

"I'm going to think about it," he said. "The Lord will guide my decision."

*     *     *

Wednesday, August 10, at exactly 2:00.

Alice picked up her phone and dialed the number. The secretary answered, announced Alice, and put the call through.

"So," said Jacques Laborie, "what is the question that's been bothering you?"

Alice smiled. Picking up a conversation where they'd left off a few weeks before was rather surreal.

"Well, you explained the initial explosion, the Big Bang, the formation of the stars and the planets, the beginnings of life coming from the stars and their combustion, but I've been wondering about a very specific point. I've often heard scientists tell religious people that God did not create the universe, because it started with the Big Bang."

"Yes."

"Fine. The Big Bang created the universe. So my question is: who created the Big Bang?"

The physicist started to laugh. "I see what you're getting at. But if you're trying to find a God somewhere, you'd be better off looking at what happened just *after* the Big Bang."

"After?"

"I would say there is where you might catch a glimpse of a mystery that might allow certain hypotheses."

"I'm intrigued."

"I explained to you last time that life emerged from fragments of stars that grouped together."

"Yes, and because of that, we're all stardust."

"Exactly. You must understand that if there hadn't been any stars, there wouldn't be any life. The universe created by the Big Bang would have been sterile."

"I see."

"So it's better to concentrate on what made the formation of stars possible in the universe."

"Okay."

"And then, we must realize that it was necessary for certain conditions to come together during the creation of the universe, conditions that are extremely precise."

"All right."

"It's a matter of the properties of the universe. It was necessary for the universe to have *very* particular, *very* specific properties. Otherwise, stars would not have appeared."

"And what determines the properties of the universe?"

"Certain factors, like the amount of dark matter, the rate of the initial expansion, the mass of protons, the speed of light, the mass of electrons, the gravitational constant, and many others."

"All right."

"It was absolutely necessary that each of those factors come together in an extremely precise way for the universe to have the necessary properties to create stars."

"Okay."

"It is as if there had to be an ultra-fine calibration of each of the factors, because if a single one of them had been slightly different, even by an infinitesimal amount, then the conditions would not have been fulfilled. And as I said: no stars, no life."

Alice thought for a moment. "So the question that comes to mind is, who did the calibrating?"

"Exactly!"

"Couldn't it be possible that it was...chance? There's the Big Bang, the explosion, and hey, presto! By sheer luck, the universe suddenly appears with all the properties necessary to form the stars: the right amount of dark matter, the right rate of expansion, the correct mass for protons, and all the rest?"

"It's possible."

"But? I sense you aren't convinced."

He took a deep breath. "It would have been sufficient for a single one the factors determining the properties of the universe to change by a hair for the conditions not to be met, and for the stars and life to never have appeared. You have to understand that it's a question of an extremely precise calibration."

Alice thought about it and acquiesced. "And what is the probability for such a calibration to have happened by chance?"

"Something on the order of ten to the power of minus sixty. If you changed a single figure up to the sixtieth decimal point, everything would be lost: no stars, no life. The void."

Alice fell silent, deep in thought.

"My famous colleague Trinh Xuan Thuan uses an image to illustrate this probability of ten to the power of minus sixty, that life came about by chance," Jacques Laborie continued. "It's the probability of an archer hitting a one-centimeter-square target placed deep in the universe, fourteen billion light-years away."

# 26

Standing by the font, an intrigued Germaine watched the line of parishioners in front of the confessional.

"This is crazy," she said.

"I never in all my life would have imagined seeing the church so full," said Cornélie.

"Did you think you'd see it after you died?"

"You're making fun of me," whined Cornélie.

Germaine looked someone new up and down, a man in his thirties.

"There are even people we don't know."

Cornélie made a face. "It was better when it was just us."

Germaine frowned and jutted her chin toward the confessional. "I wonder why so many people like it. I'm not convinced by what I've been told."

Cornélie nodded. "I'd like to be a fly on the wall."

Germaine looked at her friend and thought she looked more like a fat rat.

"If only I could slip inside," Cornélie continued, "without being seen."

"Start on a diet right away."

A woman came out of the confessional laughing out loud.

Germaine watched her walk up the side aisle.

"It's not normal," she said, shaking her head. "Religion shouldn't make you laugh."

"You think?"

"We must be like Jesus."

Cornélie slowly raised her eyes toward Christ on the cross, then half-heartedly agreed, sighing with a contrite air.

The woman, all smiles, passed them as she left the church.

Germaine was torn between her disapproval and the curiosity that was eating her up.

"I have an idea! You go to confession. That way, we'll really know what's going on."

Cornélie went pale. "Oh no! I wouldn't dare."

"What have you got to lose? Go on, go!"

"I wouldn't have the courage. You could go yourself."

"But I . . . I have nothing to feel guilty about."

Cornélie shrugged, then dropped her shoulders in resignation. "Well, you would only have to talk about our little vice."

Germaine frowned. "What vice?"

"You know very well."

"No, I don't."

"The little gossipy things we say . . . When we tell people what we think of others."

"That's not gossip. It's opening their eyes."

Cornélie was silent as her brain took in the information. "Well, in that case, pretend you think it's a vice. In any case, you shouldn't worry: it's anonymous."

"Oh, really? He'll recognize my voice!"

"He's sworn to secrecy."

Germaine made a face. It was something to think about.

★   ★   ★

Alice took the little note Sister IKEA handed her. The nun was looking at her with bright eyes, full of kindness. She smiled back. With at least a dozen others in her handbag, Alice was used to this little ritual, though its meaning still escaped her.

She unfolded it as she was leaving the church, feeling a little like a kid opening a prize from a cereal box in the hope of finding something she needed for her collection. Except that she already had the complete set.

Blinded by the intense sunlight that hit her as she came out of the semidarkness, she had difficulty making out the scribbled words.

> Jesus said: Whoever knows the all, but is deprived of himself, is deprived of everything.

She reread the message three times, with an odd sensation. Those words did not come from the Gospels. She was certain of it.

All around her, the square was empty. The tourists must have taken shelter from the heat at the beginning of the afternoon, cooling down in a tearoom or the caves at Azé or Blanot.

She went back to her father's house and connected her laptop to the internet. She typed in the message and started her search. Several sites reproduced it identically. All of them cited the same course: the Gospel of Thomas.

She'd never heard of it.

Alice then felt some doubt. She took the notes that the

deaf-mute had previously given her out of her bag and spread them out on the desk in front of her. One by one, she reread the sayings of Jesus that the nun had copied out. Did they really come from the Gospels of the Bible as she had thought? It seemed so.

She hesitated, then, to be sure, she typed the words from one of the pieces of paper into the search engine: "Blessed are you when you are hated and persecuted. Wherever you have been persecuted they will find no place," and hit the RETURN key.

The Gospel of Thomas.

*Let's see . . .*

She picked up her Bible, skimmed through different passages from the four Gospels, and found what she was looking for. The meaning was the same in each of them, but the words were different.

She did the same thing with the sayings on the other hand-written bits of paper. Each time, the meaning was similar, which explained her confusion, but the words were different.

Alice took a deep breath as she looked out the window at her father's garden. The tall bignonia in blossom clung to the old stone wall.

All the little notes from the deaf-mute came from the Gospel of Thomas, which she hadn't known existed up until then. She did some research on the internet and quickly found its origins.

In 1945, near Nag Hammadi, in Upper Egypt, someone had found, by chance, an old earthenware urn in a cave. It contained fifty-three manuscripts in a dozen papyrus notebooks that archeologists call "codices." One of them was the Gospel of Thomas, written in Coptic, a language that was similar to ancient Egyptian hieroglyphics. Archeologists were already aware of the existence of such a Gospel, as a few fragments had been discovered in the digs at Oxyrhynchus (modern al-Bahnasa), another Egyptian site, which had first been explored in 1896. The manuscript discovered at Nag Hammadi was said to be a second-century reproduction of the original text, which was written in the first century.

According to historians, it contains elements that predate the writings known as the canonical Gospels, that is, the ones officially recognized by the church.

Alice continued her research and found that Thomas, one of Jesus's twelve apostles, was believed to have brought Christianity to the area now known as Syria, in the Edessa region. A Christian community was said to have been established there by one of his disciples. The community believed faith to be a way of living, a path, and not a dogma.

*A way of living, a path.* That was exactly how Alice understood the words of Christ.

At the time, the Vatican chose to declare the Gospel of Thomas apocryphal, that is, unauthenticated, even though years later during an open meeting, Pope Benedict XVI timidly reminded everyone of its importance. What could be the reason for the church's rejection?

She found a copy of the Gospel of Thomas online. Since Jesus wrote nothing down during his lifetime, all the words attributed to him were reported by his disciples or those close to them, which explains the differences due to memory or interpretation, since each person's understanding was influenced, in spite of himself, by his own concerns, convictions, and beliefs.

The four canonical Gospels—Matthew, Mark, Luke, and John—each recount the life of Jesus as seen through the eyes of their authors. Matthew and John were disciples of Christ. Mark and Luke, who were close to his disciples, never met Jesus. The four versions are very similar, especially Mark and Matthew.

Alice found the Gospel of Thomas very different. It was not a history of the life of Jesus. There were no anecdotes in it, no miracles, nothing about how he was condemned to death, nothing about his resurrection. This Gospel simply reported Christ's words in their raw form, without embellishments or commentaries.

As soon as she started reading, Alice felt shaken. These words made her think of the sayings of the Eastern masters—obscure and sometimes paradoxical—whose meaning was not immediately clear but which mysteriously awakened something within us.

When she had finished, she leaned back in her armchair and looked out the window at the flowers, the birds, the clouds, for a long time.

What was obvious in reading this Gospel was that Jesus seemed to have a non-dualistic vision that matched up quite well with that of Lao Tzu and Eastern spiritual masters, in opposition to the dualistic vision the church ascribed to him, a dualistic vision that separates people from the rest of the world, and separates them from God.

In this Gospel, Jesus invites us to be introspective, to know ourselves, and he stresses that God is also within us.

*Within us.* But then, why did he say the opposite in the canonical Gospels? Alice remembered that a few weeks before she had checked the wording he used on the subject. When replying to a group of Pharisees who were asking him when the kingdom of God will come, he had replied unambiguously, "It is among you," and not "in you." Why the contradiction? Had one of the evangelists made a mistake when transcribing Christ's words, or had Jesus been inconsistent?

Alice sighed, deep in thought. She watched a swallow singing on the branch of a cherry tree in the garden, opposite three others perched in a row along the clothesline. She smiled, thinking that the bird was perhaps delivering some spiritual message to the other birds, a message that the others would still be transmitting two thousand years later, perhaps distorting it a little! She would have liked to be able to translate its language.

This made her want to verify that Jesus's "among you" was not the result of a bad translation. She found the passage in question: verse 21 from chapter 17 in the Gospel of Luke. A few clicks were enough for her to find online the main translations of the Bible, the most well-known and circulated ones.

In the Jerusalem Bible, Alice was disappointed to find the same expression: "among you." Then she noticed a footnote that stated, "Also sometimes translated as 'within you,' but this does not seem to be indicated by the context." *Well, well . . .*

She continued looking.

The very respected Holman Christian Standard Bible also used "among you," but with an asterisk pointing to a footnote that Alice was eager to read: "Also sometimes translated as 'within you,' but this translation unfortunately makes the kingdom of God a reality that is only internal and private."

She surfed the net until she found a site that published the original Greek version of the Gospel of Luke, found verse 21, and saw the expression used: *"entòs umôn estin."*

She checked several translation sites. They all translated it as "it is within you."

Fearing it might just be an approximation, she searched further for the word *"entos"* and learned that it meant not only "within" but one's most profound inner being.

Alice collapsed back in her chair.

It was quite simply incredible.

The translators had deliberately replaced "within you" with "among you" because the idea upset them.

Monumental.

Alice had thought that each evangelist might have accidentally distorted Christ's words through the biased filter of his understanding. But for translators to intentionally alter the words was beyond belief. And, of course, that changed everything.

The more a non-dualistic vision seemed likely, a vision in which each one of us, stardust, might be a fragment of the whole and thus a fragment of God, the closer Alice came to a concept that she felt she could adhere to—even if she didn't quite know how to define the idea of "God": A creative force? A communal conscience, of which each of us carries a fragment?

These badly translated words of Jesus made her think that other elements of his language or view of life might have been altered in the same way. How could she know?

Alice returned to her keyboard, searched some more, but in vain. There was so much written about the Bible that it was impossible to find anything quickly without narrowing down her search.

She immediately thought of Raphaël Duvernet. The expert on Eastern religions probably had connections with specialists on Christianity. Of course.

She picked up her phone, dialed the château, and insisted to his entourage that she had to speak to him. She pictured him in his wine cellar, in his Louis XIII armchair on the enormous Persian rug, surrounded by casks, good bottles of wine, and dirty glasses, having given strict instructions that he wasn't to be disturbed. But her public relations experience won over their resistance, and, in the distance, she finally heard the familiar, laughably aggressive voice of the disgraced expert.

"What the hell does she want from me now?" she heard him say as he got closer to the phone.

She couldn't help laughing.

"What do you want this time?" he said bluntly.

"Your address book," she said as calmly as could be.

"I've never known a woman with such nerve."

But he agreed.

# 27

THE LITTLE ROAD WEAVED ITS WAY ALONG THE MOUNTAINSIDE. Dark clouds were quickly gathering in the changeable sky at the end of the day. Alice would arrive well before night fell. She just hoped the storm wouldn't start before she got back. She could have waited until the next day to see Jeremy in the church or at home without rushing, but Théo had gone to bed early. Best take advantage of an evening of freedom.

A broken-down tractor blocked access to the top of Suin Mountain. She left her car at the side of the road and crossed the Morphée Woods on foot. Scattered here and there were large, strange stones that seemed to have fallen from the sky. When she came out of the woods, she took the path that led up to the sweet-scented moor, amid the broom bushes and pale heather. Nearly six hundred meters up, the air was much cooler than in the valley.

She soon noticed the statue of the Virgin Mary, high on the

summit. As she got closer, she recognized Jeremy in the distance, standing with his back to her.

Beneath the dim, yellowish rays of the fading sun, his black cassock stood out against the sky. Clusters of dark clouds seemed eager to reach Mont Blanc, beyond the horizon. Muted by the wind, the sound of the Romanesque church's bells reached her from down below.

She moved closer. Jeremy turned around and watched her walk over to him, his face impassive.

"I stopped by your mother's," she said, out of breath. "She told me you'd be here."

He didn't reply, simply watched her with kind detachment as her hair flew around in the wind. She caught her breath, admiring the view from so high up. In every direction, valleys, hills, wooded countryside, and forests stretched out to infinity, disappearing far beyond the horizon.

They walked a little in silence, side by side, toward the rocks that leaned against each other at the very top of the hill, just below the statue.

"Someone told me an old Hindu legend," she said. "It's about a time when all men were gods. But men abused their divinity so much that Brahma, the god of creation, decided to take their divinity away from them and hide it in a place where they could never find it. The lesser gods suggested burying it in a deep grave, but Brahma replied that men would dig and dig until they found it. The bottom of the ocean? No, they would eventually dive down and take it back. The lesser gods admitted they couldn't think of anything else—no place existed where human beings weren't capable of finding it someday. Then Brahma said: 'We will hide divinity in the deepest part of man himself, for that is the only place he would never go to seek it.' The legend concluded that from that day onward, man explored the entire world and the depths of the ocean, looking for something that lived within him."

Jeremy smiled and said nothing.

They took a few more steps, hoisted themselves up onto one of the rocks, and sat down with their feet hanging over the edge. In the distance, toward the Loire Valley to the west, a bolt of lightning silently zigzagged across the sky.

"I've found the Gospel of Thomas. In that Gospel, Jesus has a non-dualistic vision that is very different from the church's doctrine."

Jeremy remained calm, smiling slightly.

"So I immediately did some research," she said. "I've just spoken to a few experts I've gotten in touch with, passionate people whose voices are rarely heard. And I learned some things that I was totally unaware of before. It seems that the church, from its very beginnings, did everything it could to block out the non-dualistic view and present God as an external entity. In the canonical Gospels, Jesus's words were adapted for that meaning. Even the Protestants, who had always been respectful of biblical writings, thought it right to add things. In the Lord's Prayer, the only words Jesus dictated to his apostles, they deliberately put at the end: 'For thine is the kingdom, the power, and the glory, forever and ever.'"

Jeremy said nothing. Alice looked up at the statue of the Virgin. She could smell the approaching storm in the air.

"The church probably completely invented the dogma of Mary's virginity to emphasize the idea of an all-powerful external God. The problem is that Jesus had sisters and four brothers, who are discussed in the Gospels: James, Joseph, Simon, and Jude. Hard to remain a virgin with all those children. So the church officially renamed them 'cousins,' to preserve the dogma, and that still remains the official position today."

221

Jeremy did not react.

"And yet," Alice continued, "man's divinity, which the Hindu legend puts forward, is found all over the planet. In Judaism, it is written in the Psalms, 'You are gods.' The Buddhists say, 'We are the consciences of Buddha.' And Jesus himself said, 'I and the Father are one,' after having affirmed that his Father is also ours. That caused him to be charged by the Jews with blasphemy and condemned to death. To top it all off, while acting in his name, the church has never stopped accusing of blasphemy anyone who adopted that non-dualistic view. You taught me about Meister Eckhart, the great Dominican mystic of the Middle Ages. I found out that the church put him before the court of the Inquisition for having revealed his view of man's divinity to the public. The pope himself condemned him."

Jeremy continued listening to her in silence. Alice was surprised that he didn't seem annoyed or even surprised by her words.

"Jesus," she continued, "went so far as to affirm that each of us could carry out miracles: 'I tell you, whoever believes in me will do the works I have been doing, and they will do even greater things than these.' And you see, Jeremy, the thing that troubled me the most was realizing the meaning of the words he said to his disciples: 'Therefore I tell you, whatever you ask for in prayer, believe that you have received it, and it will be yours.' The translators preferred to change the end to say it 'will be granted to you,' implying there was an external, all-powerful God. What strikes me is that Jesus doesn't say 'believe that you will receive it,' a hope for some time in the future, but 'believe that you have received it,' affirming that reality will conform to our perception of it. It's obviously surprising and a little upsetting for anyone with a rational mind. I've thought about it a lot over the past few days, and I think I've found a way out: let's assume that God exists—"

"That doesn't take a lot of effort on my part, you know."

Alice laughed. "If I hope to obtain something, the formulation of that thought presupposes that I do not have the thing in question: if I want it, it means I don't have it. So 'I don't have it' is the message I am sending to God. Conversely, if I believe I have received it, if I succeed in believing I have it, then that is the message sent to God. So perhaps God conforms to my visions, because God . . . is within me. If I am a fragment of God, then there is a creative force in me. A creative force that makes my thoughts concrete, that makes real what I believe is real. Perhaps that is also the reason why Buddha said we create the world with our thoughts. And you remember our personal development seminars with Toby Collins? To help us realize our dreams, he advised us to act as if we already had the ability to do so."

The dark clouds moved en masse toward Beaujolais, revealing to the west a golden sky tinted the color of cognac, allowing the sun to cast, here and there, a shimmering bright light over the wooded countryside. Some large birds of prey hovered calmly above, masters of the sky, their black shapes standing out against the natural scene below.

Sitting on the edge of the rock at the top of the mountain, legs swinging in space and her face caressed by a breeze that smelled of rain, Alice felt she was sitting up in the first balcony watching a spectacle of startling immensity.

"This view of a God within brings with it a mixture of self-confidence and confidence in life," said Alice. "Perhaps that's what faith is."

Jeremy smiled. "If we were in the Middle Ages, that view would mainly cause my superiors to tie you to a stake and burn you as a heretic!"

Alice burst out laughing again. "The idea of confidence, of faith, that creates reality reminds me of the Bible story of Jesus walking on water. The first time I read it, I laughed my head off, but if you get used to the idea of the supernatural, there's something interesting about it. I can't remember the exact words, but—"

"'The boat was already a considerable distance from land, buffeted by the waves because the wind was against it,'" Jeremy began reciting from memory. "'Shortly before dawn, Jesus went out to them, walking on the lake. When the disciples saw him walking on the lake, they were terrified. "It's a ghost!" they said, and cried out in fear. But Jesus immediately said to them: "Take courage! It is I. Do not be afraid." "Lord, if it is you," Peter replied, "tell me to come to you on the water." "Come," he said. Then Peter got down out of the boat, walked on the water, and came toward Jesus. But when he saw the wind, he was afraid and, beginning to sink, cried out, "Lord, save me!" Immediately Jesus reached out his hand and caught him. "You of little faith," he said, "why did you doubt?" And when they climbed into the boat, the wind died down.'"

"That's it. Jesus doesn't say that supernatural power comes from an external divine force. He insinuates it comes from a state of confidence. As soon as Peter doubts, he loses his power."

One after the other, two lightning bolts struck between the dark clouds near Beaujolais. The storm was heading south.

"In the Gospel of Thomas," she continued, "Jesus gives another means of finding that power: 'But if you do not know yourselves, then you dwell in poverty, and you are poverty.' In other words, self-knowledge helps to free us from the ego, and unless we do that, we have no power."

Alice looked out into the distance.

Wings outstretched, a falcon carried by the wind rapidly flew past, seemingly effortlessly, as if he were gliding between the clouds and the sky.

"That view of internal divinity also gives me the feeling that there is a dimension in which the notion of time does not exist," said Alice, "something that certain physicists are working on proving. Perhaps I exist outside of time, and my incarnation in this body is not essential. The stardust that I am, that fragment of the whole, might exist in another reality beyond this temporal, earthly world. By freeing myself from my ego, which separates me from other people and from everything, I emerge from the duality, and by leaving that duality, I leave temporality. 'Before Abraham was born, I am!' Jesus said. What I had taken as a mistake in verb tenses is perhaps actually the most profound and troubling sentence of all."

The storm began to move farther south, gradually revealing the sky. On top of the hill, the wind was dying down a little.

Alice looked at Jeremy. "When I told you about the Gospel of Thomas, you didn't ask me how I'd found out about it."

He didn't reply, but she thought she could see the beginnings of a smile on his impassive face.

"*You're* the one who directed the deaf-mute nun! Admit it!"

He sighed, then smiled. "You made me promise never to talk to you about God. I kept my promise."

"But...does that mean you share this view of man's divine nature?"

Jeremy sat still for a moment.

Then he made a face.

Finally, slowly, he assented.

"Well, then, I really wonder why you continue to belong to this church, which has done everything it could to fight against that view."

"I don't belong to a church, Alice, I belong to God. It's

225

the ego that pushes someone to consider themselves Catholic, Buddhist, or Muslim. The ego seeks to belong to one camp to stand out from the others, to cause rifts. Every true spiritual force, on the contrary, aims to be free of the affiliations, the identifications of the ego, so it can be linked to others, to the universe, to God."

As she took the path back to her car, Alice thought back to Jesus's supernatural powers. Ever since she had read Campbell and his analyses of hundreds of myths from all over the world, she couldn't help but see, in the events of Jesus's life, a mythology that carried messages. Except that Jesus, unlike mythological characters, was a historical figure, a man who had truly lived. And yet she obviously found it difficult to take literally that he had cured the blind and the crippled, brought the dead back to life, been resurrected. Her rational mind found it difficult to believe in the supernatural, and she couldn't help seeing in those events stories that had been invented to emphasize Christ's messages.

When we read in the Bible that Jesus cured the blind, how could we not see an illustration of his desire to open our eyes? He told the cripples to pick up their bags, stand up, and walk. Was he not asking us to take responsibility for our lives? When he raised the dead, was that not a call for us to awaken, to realize that living only on the materialistic plane was the same as not living at all? If we are told of his death and resurrection, is that not to invite us to die and be reborn, meaning to extinguish our ego to allow our divine nature to blossom?

Either his disciples had embellished his story with imagined events in order to emphasize their master's message—in which case it was astonishing that pious men would lie to that extent, since the Bible affirms that liars are banished from God's presence—or Jesus had truly carried out miracles, his life unfolding to illustrate his messages right to the end. And if that were the case, he couldn't have been a simple human being.

"I," he said, "am the way and the truth and the life."

# 28

Jeremy stretched his legs out diagonally in the confessional to relax them. He could hear the curtain being opened next to him.

"Father, I have come to confess . . . my gossiping."

He couldn't help but smile when he heard the familiar voice of the elderly woman, whose contrition sounded somewhat forced.

"Tell me, my child, what are you feeling guilty about?"

"Guilty?"

Her voice suddenly sounded confident again.

"Let's say," she continued, "that I sometimes think it necessary to alert parishioners to the misdeeds of others, when I should, perhaps, leave them alone in their naivete."

"I understand."

"You see, some people let themselves be fooled. Their eyes need to be opened!"

"My child, Jesus said, 'Consider carefully what you hear. With the measure you use, it will be measured to you.'"

"But . . . I only reveal actions that are contrary to Christian charity!"

"My child, do you come to confess your sins or justify them?"

As she did not reply, he added, "Saint John said, 'Anyone who claims to be in the light but hates a brother or sister is still in the darkness.'"

She said nothing.

He remembered the penance proposed one day by the Curé of Ars to one of his female parishioners who had confessed to being a gossip.

"This is what you are going to do, my child: go and ask for a bag of feathers from the Cannata farmyard and spill them out in the middle of the ruins of the abbey. Then go back to the same place the next day and pick them all up."

"All the feathers? But that's impossible! They will have all been blown away by the wind. I'll never get them back!"

Jeremy remained silent, allowing her to reflect on her own words.

She left, mumbling that it was much simpler when she was asked to say the Lord's Prayer ten times.

\*　　\*　　\*

"It's a way of defying your authority, Your Grace."

The bishop walked the hundred paces along the row of high windows in his office. When he had a difficult decision to make, he needed to walk. Movement allowed him to think freely.

"You're certain that a date has been set to baptize the child?"

The curate confirmed it. "Sunday, August 28, at the end of Mass."

"And Father Jeremy knows that the curate from Charolles refused the family?"

"Yes, Your Grace."

"You're sure?"

"Positive."

The bishop stared at him for a few moments, then started to walk again.

When he was trying to control his irritation, the curate ended his sentences by pursing his lips, which looked like a pout.

"He's testing you, Your Grace. It's a provocation of your authority. If you don't react, nothing will stop him. And then it will be too late."

"It's never too late."

"There are many parishioners behind him. More and more of them. Wait any longer and they'll make him into a saint. Then your hands will be tied and you'll be obliged to accept him. He'll be a thorn in your side forever."

The bishop sat down at his desk. The priest was staring at him with an anxious look on his face. He wasn't wrong. Madame de Sirdegault herself had warned him twice in the past. Though he hadn't seen her in a long time since then.

"He could get away with anything, Your Grace."

The bishop sighed.

"He must be sanctioned," said the curate. "Then calm will return to the parish of Cluny."

The bishop hesitated. How would a sanction be seen by the other priests? Would that confirm his power or discredit him?

"Think of everything he's dared to do in the space of a few months," stressed the curate. "Allow him to keep going and he'll become uncontrollable. The Holy See would call us back to order in vain, and we'd be seen as incompetent."

The bishop twisted his amethyst ring around and around.

He was beginning to grow weary of the problems coming from Cluny. His patience mustn't turn into indecision, or sooner or later he would pay the consequences.

\* \* \*

The man waited patiently in line. It was actually the first time he had seen a line for a confessional. He had never been to confession himself. Or to church, for that matter. Except sometimes, for concerts. And the only times he had prayed were when his father had been seriously ill, then his mother, and then only out of desperation. But his cousin had insisted so much that she finally convinced him to make the trip from Mâcon.

When it was his turn, he slipped into the narrow space and closed the curtain behind him. He had the impression that he was in a photo booth. Except there was no stool. Just a kind of badly installed bench just above floor level. He had to bend over to sit down, and then felt a shelf digging into his shoulder blades. Pretty basic, comfort-wise. But given that it was free, you couldn't be too demanding. At least he wasn't falling asleep as he did on the couch at the shrink's he'd gone to see once, years before.

"I'm listening, my son."

"Hello, monsieur, I've come to see you because I'm having a problem with my upstairs neighbor. I live in an apartment building in Mâcon, and my neighbor looks down on me—he totally snubs me. I feel bad as soon as I leave my place because if I run into him, it's going to put me in a bad mood for the rest of the day. And what's even worse is that we have the same schedule. We see each other almost every day."

"Tell me a little more about the situation."

"Oh, it's simple—I often go up in the elevator with him. He

231

lives one floor up. He speaks to me in a condescending way. I can tell that he looks down on me, that he thinks he's better than me, much better, even."

"You're not responsible for what other people think."

"But he shouldn't think he's better!"

"That's his problem, not yours."

"But it's very unpleasant. It makes me furious!"

"And that's your problem."

"What do you mean?"

"His feeling superior is *his* problem. You can't do anything about that—you're not his shrink. The fact that it upsets you, that's *your* problem."

There was silence as the man thought about what those words meant. "But . . . it's normal to feel bad. I'm not made of stone."

"Does the fact that this person thinks he's superior to you change your worth?"

"No, of course not."

"So what *does* it change?"

He gave him time to think about it.

"Perhaps . . . my perception of my worth," he admitted.

"It's because you're not sufficiently convinced of your worth that you're sensitive to other people's opinions of you."

"Perhaps."

"And if this neighbor behaves so haughtily, can you guess what the reason for that might be?"

"No idea."

"It's probably because he also doubts his worth. And in that case, he has the same problem as you. It's just that his ego manifests it differently. Should you hold it against someone who is suffering the same as you?"

"He might be suffering as much, but I don't take it out on anyone."

"Maybe."

"You don't believe me?"

"We're not always aware of how we unwillingly hurt other people."

"All right. So what's the solution in the present case, with the guy who looks down on me?"

"If someone else's ego touches you, and you respond to that ego, you're reinforcing it. If you manage to see beyond the ego and speak to that person, you will free that person from his prison. In relationships, someone else's ego is a cell whose bars disappear when you manage to see the person behind them."

The man sighed. "But what should I do, practically speaking?"

The priest waited a few moments before replying.

"Jesus said: 'Do unto others what you would have them do unto you.'"

The next evening, the man came home from his office and ran into the neighbor from upstairs. He was standing in front of the mailboxes at the entrance to the building. The man said hello, trying to sound friendly. The neighbor looked him up and down, raised his chin, and grudgingly deigned to give him a brief "Good evening," as nasty as could be.

*If you respond to his ego, you're reinforcing it.*

The man decided to give him a particularly cheerful smile.

The neighbor quickly looked away.

They entered the wooden cage of the old elevator, and the internal sliding door slowly closed, then the heavy wrought-iron door slammed shut on them.

The man turned toward his neighbor, who was staring at some invisible spot on the ceiling as the elevator crawled up ever so slowly. Their proximity weighed on them, as did the silence that surrounded them.

The man started to talk quietly and was anxious to hear his words echo, breaking the silence.

"I went to church yesterday..."

He immediately felt his neighbor tense up and stare even more intently at the ceiling.

"And I prayed for you," he continued.

The other man's eyes widened, still staring at the invisible spot, as if he had been hypnotized by some magic words.

Silence fell again, but the words continued to echo. The old wheezy elevator continued to rise with difficulty.

"I prayed that people might manage to see your kindness behind the mask of your appearance."

He saw his neighbor's lips begin to tremble, as if he were muttering something, but no sound emerged.

The elevator stopped at his floor, and the doors creaked open.

The man got out, turned around, and added, "Because *I* know that deep down, you're a good person."

The neighbor never looked down on him again.

# 29

Sitting at the table in the garden in the shade of the old walnut tree, a plate of hot madeleine cakes and a steaming teapot in front of her, Alice was engrossed in her Bible.

"Come and have some madeleines," she called out to Théo.

Hard to compete with the swings.

"Otherwise I'll eat them all and gain four pounds," she added, more quietly.

She tore the shredded *Civil Code* cover off the Bible.

She was excited about what she had just understood. Jesus gave an essential path to liberate oneself from the ego, which she had never realized until then. She already had in mind the theme of Jeremy's next sermon.

She heard the sound of footsteps and turned around.

"Hi! I was just thinking about you!" she said as he came over to her. "I have a suggestion for next Sunday's Mass. Have a seat."

He sat down, and she offered him the plate of madeleines, which he declined.

He waved in a friendly way to Théo and looked all around him at the garden, as if he wanted to savor the sight of it. He finally looked back at her and smiled, a smile full of kindness and...something she thought was a hint of sadness.

"Is something wrong, Jeremy?"

He continued smiling with kindness, but she could sense that he was trying to prolong the moment of lightheartedness, which worried her even more. When he finally spoke, his voice was calm and controlled.

"That will be my last Mass in Cluny."

"What? But...why?"

"I'm being sent to Yaoundé."

Alice looked at him, incredulous, before truly taking in the meaning of his words.

She was speechless.

It was as if everything were suddenly falling to pieces. Everything they had done, everything they had set in motion, all the efforts to attract parishioners, everything that had benefited so many people.

She immediately felt overcome with sadness, disappointment, disgust.

"Why? Why are they doing it?"

He didn't reply.

"But...do they have the right to ship you off to Cameroon just like that, with no warning?"

He shrugged his shoulders and nodded. He was powerless. "The bishop reminded me that the apostles were always on the move."

"And everything we've accomplished here?"

"A new priest will be appointed."

"Who will undo everything."

"Not necessarily."

She was crushed.

"The idea that they're going to put back those silly little songs and all the rest makes me so depressed. They're going to send everyone running."

"We can't know that, Alice."

She shook her head in disgust. "When exactly are you leaving?"

"Thursday morning at dawn. The curate of the diocese is picking me up at the rectory to drive me to the airport in Geneva."

"Thursday? Why so soon?"

"It's probably necessary. I'll know more on Sunday morning. I've been told to go to the diocese before Mass."

She had great difficulty in imagining that soon he wouldn't be there, that they would see each other only rarely. The parishioners would also miss him, that was certain.

"The family from Charolles is very lucky that the baptism has been set for Sunday. A week later and it wouldn't have happened. And it's so very important to them."

"Yes, that was my impression."

"In any case, it's not fair of them to transfer you at the very moment when all the fruits of your labors are being reaped!"

He sighed, then smiled calmly. "The essential thing—more than reaping the fruits ourselves—is that we acted from our hearts and consciences, Alice. Jesus said: 'Do not let your left hand know what your right hand is doing.'"

"I guess I haven't attained that level of wisdom."

He looked at her with eyes full of kindness. "Who knows the exact significance of our actions? Who knows what we will have learned from this experience? Things sometimes seem to escape us in life, but it's just that, at that moment, we are unaware of the deeper meaning."

*  *  *

Germaine held her shopping bag against her stomach as she crossed the market square.

"Throw feathers around—that's just black magic!"

"It's hardly believable," said Cornélie. "If anyone had told me we'd see that in Cluny, well, really . . ."

"Jesus did say there would be false prophets."

"That's true," said Cornélie.

Germaine lowered her voice. "Father Jeremy is a servant of the devil!"

"Hush! You're scaring me."

"It's not surprising that he's leaving for Africa. He must be going there to meet up with voodoo sorcerers."

"Oh my God!"

"Right from the start, I said you had to be careful of him. Right from the start!"

"At least we weren't taken in," said Cornélie. "And it's not as though we didn't warn the others."

"Take Madame de Sirdegault. She defended him the other day!"

"Before, she was a good woman."

"He must have cast a spell on her!"

"The poor thing."

Germaine nodded her head in agreement. Suddenly she froze, stopping Cornélie by putting her arm in front of her.

"Look who's over there!"

On the other side of the square, Father Jeremy was walking down the Rue de la République in his long, jet-black cassock.

"My God," said Cornélie, making the sign of the cross.

Germaine kept very calm, grabbed her crucifix, held it out in the direction of the priest, and murmured in a solemn voice, *"Vade retro, Satana!"*

# 30

WHEN SHE ARRIVED IN FRONT OF THE CHURCH, ALICE ALREADY felt very nostalgic.

There were a few more people than before standing outside, like every week. The atmosphere was joyful and care-free. Most people had probably not yet heard about Jeremy's departure.

The morning sun lit up the medieval facades along the square, making their stones glisten. Most of the windows were still wide open, in the hope that the final moments of the day's coolness would waft in.

She greeted the familiar faces and went into the church to meet Jeremy. The parishioners were already sitting in their seats, especially the older ones, who feared that the newcomers might take their places.

She saw the couple from Charolles, sitting on a bench next to the baptismal font with a little boy of seven or eight, the baby in his father's arms. They were surrounded by people, probably their family and friends. The parents stood up and walked over to her, their eyes shining.

"We want to thank you again. It's thanks to you that he will be baptized today."

"You're welcome."

She crossed the nave. Jeremy wasn't there yet. The sacristy was empty. The interview with the bishop must have gone on a bit.

She walked back down the side aisle to go outside. At the entrance, many conversations were going on at once. There was a certain lightness in the air, and Alice found it difficult to believe that this would be the last time they would gather together for Jeremy's Mass.

But when was he going to get there?

★   ★   ★

"I've done my best to keep him here, but now, Your Grace, I think it's best you see him. Otherwise I can't be responsible for what happens."

Sitting behind his large gilt desk, the bishop raised one eyebrow. "Show him in."

The curate went out into the antechamber.

"I have to go," said Father Jeremy to the curate. "Please send my apologies to the bishop and tell him I must carry out my obligations to my parishioners. I'm happy to come back after Mass if he wishes. Let me know."

He was already walking away when the curate touched his arm. "Wait."

"I can't wait any longer."

"His Grace will see you now," said the curate.

Father Jeremy hesitated for a moment. "I'm terribly sorry, but I don't have any more time."

He had already turned toward the exit when the bishop's voice called out from his office.

"Come in, Father Jeremy!"

The priest froze.

"Follow me," the curate whispered.

They went into the office.

"Sit down, Father Jeremy," said the bishop as he took his place in the enormous armchair at the end of the long rectangular table.

The curate stepped away to discreetly stand near the window next to the door.

"Unfortunately, I'm not going to be able to stay, Your Grace, because the Mass at Cluny starts in—"

"Relax. We have all the time in the world. I'm sorry I was late, but it is absolutely necessary that you are prepared for your departure."

"But I'm expected at ten o'clock for Mass."

"Don't worry about that. We'll say it was an emergency. Everyone will understand."

The priest did not reply.

The curate breathed a sigh of relief.

The Mass would not take place. No farewell speeches or displays of emotion. The diocese would not be responsible for creating a martyr.

Better to nip it in the bud and move on.

*　　*　　*

10:15.

Jeremy's delay was becoming embarrassing.

Alice had been sure that the meeting with the bishop before morning Mass was a bad idea. She noticed a nun among the parishioners and walked over to her.

"Father Jeremy isn't here," she said quietly. "Go to the rectory and call the bishopric and ask them what time he left."

The nun seemed to hesitate for a moment, then obeyed.

People were looking at their watches and showing signs of impatience. Everyone had come in from outside, and the church was filling up.

The elderly Victor came over to her. He had learned that Jeremy was leaving and was appalled. He started naming all the priests who had been there before Jeremy. But Alice wasn't listening to him. She was too worried about the absence of her friend. She hoped nothing had happened to him on his way back.

10:25.

The nun finally came back. "Father Jeremy has been detained at the bishopric," she said. "Mass has been canceled, and I've been told to tell the parishioners."

"Mass has been canceled?"

The nun nodded. She looked as though she shared Alice's disappointment. "Do you think you could...tell everyone?" she said, a pleading look on her face.

Alice agreed.

The nun disappeared in the direction of the rectory.

*Detained at the bishopric.* It couldn't have happened at a worse time. The promised baptism, the sermon that meant so much to her...

A nasty blow for everyone. Poor Jeremy couldn't even say goodbye to his flock. Calling him to the bishopric, an hour away from Cluny, on the morning of Mass was very strange. Why not the day before, in the afternoon, or the next day? And now he was being detained there. Bizarre. What if it was to prevent the baptism?

She didn't trust those people. Especially after Jeremy's arbitrary transfer. She felt they were capable of anything.

Depressed, Alice went inside the church to announce, much against her will, the bad news. She had the impression that, despite herself, she was an accomplice to the bishopric's maneuvers.

Her heart broke when she saw the family from Charolles again. She controlled herself and walked over to them.

"There's a problem," she said. "Father Jeremy has been detained at the bishopric. The Mass is being canceled."

"Canceled?" said the mother, her eyes opening wide.

"But . . . what about the baptism?" asked the father.

"I am sincerely terribly sorry for you. I'm so upset . . ."

There was such an awful look of disappointment on their faces that she didn't have the courage to tell them that Father Jeremy would not be holding any other Masses, and that the baptism would probably never take place.

"Please, do something."

Alice, powerless, looked into their pleading eyes.

They had moved heaven and earth, and she had promised them that their child would be baptized.

"I'm so terribly sorry."

She moved away and walked toward the choir. The great disappointment of these people added to her own, added to her sadness, her helplessness, her anger. She walked past the candles, whose little flames fluttered with melancholy. Her bitter sigh would be enough to put them out.

As always, when things eluded her, she felt a desire to act, to take control of the situation, not to give in to events, whether they were fortuitous or calculated by malevolent people. But in the present case, there was nothing to be done, and that increased her resentment.

When she reached the foot of the rostrum, she turned to look at the people gathered there before stepping up. The nave was three-quarters full. Her heart ached as she thought back to the first Mass she had attended, five or six months before. Twelve parishioners had been there. Today, there were two or three hundred. And there would be even more of them if all the people who attended confession were there.

How many would be left by the end of the year?

She noticed Madame de Sirdegault, sitting in her seat in the first row as always, and wondered why she looked so troubled. She also recognized Étienne, a little farther away. She glanced again at the young couple, who were watching her, their little boy on their knees, the baby in their arms, the godfather, godmother, their family and friends around them. Everyone looked defeated. They had undoubtedly organized a party, gifts, the traditional sugar-coated almonds with the date printed on the packets... everything was ruined.

Alice shook her head. This situation was unfair, no matter how you looked at it. She took a deep breath to help her nerves. The more she felt the unfairness of it, the more the desire to act grew within her, like some internal commandment.

An idea came to mind, an idea so utterly inconceivable that she immediately dismissed it.

But she then felt a kind of force rising from within her, something that was at once calling her and carrying her along with it. No. She couldn't allow herself to do it; it was unacceptable.

She felt torn, pulled between the internal call and her reason, which forbade her to follow it. She owed it to herself to be logical, to have a bit of self-control, to respect the rules as much as possible.

She then remembered that Jesus had said: "So then, because you are lukewarm, and neither cold nor hot, I will vomit you out of my mouth."

*I will vomit you out of my mouth.* She repeated the words to herself for a few seconds.

She climbed onto the platform and walked over to the microphone on the lectern.

"Hello, everyone."

She heard her voice echo throughout the church.

"I regret to inform you that Father Jeremy is being transferred. He will be leaving in a few days for a country far away. And we have just learned that he is now being detained at the bishopric."

She glanced over the entire audience. Everyone was looking at her in absolute silence.

She took a deep breath. "I'm... I'm going to say Mass in his place today."

A wave of whispers ran across the nave from every direction. A few cries of indignation as well.

She noticed the busybodies looking as if they were about to have a stroke. On top of his stone column, the sculpture of Pidou Berlu seemed even more astounded than ever.

Some people stood up and walked out, soon followed by a few others.

The situation was intimidating, especially for her, as she normally had terrible stage fright whenever she had to speak in public. But she had made the move, following the momentum that was carrying her, listening to her heart, and she decided to continue, without pretending to be a priest, without seeking to be labeled with a specific role, but simply being herself and delivering the messages she wanted to deliver, the messages she had prepared for Jeremy's sermon. Of course, she had forgotten the exact words, but again, she decided to trust her intuition, her instinct, and her heart, and not try to remember the lines written days before. Those days belonged to the past, and the truth of the moment is always greater than the truth of the past.

Besides, this was not a show. She was saying this Mass for the parishioners and not for herself, and she expected nothing in return.

She looked around at everyone who had remained. If they were there, it was to be awakened spiritually, as she herself had sought to be for several months. In the end, they were on the same quest, and she wanted to share what had begun to contribute to her own awakening. Not to keep it for herself, but to see that it benefited everyone.

As the desire to pass on what she had learned grew in her, she began to feel a kind of friendship toward the assembled people.

Then something amazing happened: her stage fright completely disappeared, vanished as if by magic. She had spent her whole life fighting against her shyness, a shyness that she skillfully hid by trying to be confident and take the lead, to the point that she appeared audacious. Now she suddenly found herself free, with no effort whatsoever. And she realized that shyness was also a product of the ego. The shy woman she had been had believed that at every moment in life, all eyes were focused on her to judge her. Wasn't that idea ... narcissistic?

By refusing to play a role or to protect herself, by not trying to stand out one way or another, by being content to express what was dear to her heart at the present moment, by putting herself aside and instead serving her cause and the messages she wanted to pass on, by sincerely turning toward the people she intended those messages for, she had freed herself of her shyness.

"My name is Alice. I'm a childhood friend of Father Jeremy's.

Even though I have often seen him doing this work, I'm not sure I know how to respect all the rules of Mass, but..."

"Do you at least believe in God?"

The booming voice cut through the peacefulness of the church and echoed in all directions. Stopped dead in her tracks, Alice looked to her left, where the question had come from. She couldn't single out the man who had asked it. From his voice, he must have been in his sixties. Probably a neighbor who knew her family history of atheism.

Embarrassed, Alice was trying to find the right words, and the fact that she didn't reply immediately caused a new wave of whispers in the church.

She looked up again in the direction of the unknown man.

"Tell me who God is and I'll tell you if I believe in him."

The sound of buzzing filled the nave again, then silence fell. Everyone had turned to look at the man.

But no reply came. The man who had been so quick to challenge Alice in her belief in God seemed incapable of saying who he was.

She took a deep breath and began.

"For a long time, I considered myself an atheist. Then I discovered the value of Jesus's words and realized he was a very wise man. I applied his precepts to experience them myself, and I was troubled by what happened to me then. I understood that they were guiding me to free myself from my ego, and the rare times that I actually managed that for a few seconds, I felt something that resembled another reality, a world in which I no longer obsessively sought to exist independently of others, a world in which, on the contrary, I felt connected to others, to the point of merging with them, with the universe, with everything. Perhaps this was catching sight for a second of what Jesus called the 'kingdom of heaven'? I have no idea.

Perhaps it was a connection to that part of divinity that exists within us.

"In fact, I have often heard that deep within us all there is sin. Today I know that isn't true: deep within us is the divine. Sin is only what leads us astray. So does God exist? For a long time I laughed at the idea of a bearded man, sitting on a cloud, gifted with exceptional powers. The Jewish people are probably right to refuse to name God. Giving a name puts images in our minds, personifying what is not a person, transforming something that is spiritual into something concrete. The simple word 'God' evokes in me a character with a palpable existence, gifted with absolute powers, who rules over everything, from births to deaths, as well as each person's destiny and the workings of the universe. And that I cannot believe in. On the other hand, there does perhaps exist a creative force, a kind of energy, a consciousness of which we are, without knowing it, an element, a fraction, a link. Just as our bodies are stardust, a fragment of the universe, our consciousness might be a fragment of a universal consciousness, of a creative force we belong to even as we believe we are detached and independent, because we each also enjoy an individual consciousness."

She looked around at the assembled believers.

"Our individual consciousness would make us forget that universal consciousness, and our egos would cut us off from it by pushing us to be disunited, separating us so we stand out as individuals."

She paused for a few seconds.

"And if that impalpable force, that creative force, that universal consciousness is called God, then God is not a powerful being external to ourselves, whom we implore to obtain favors as if we were talking to the master of the universe. Instead, it would be both a cosmic force and a force within us, to which we can connect and through which we could be reborn, as if we were returning to the fold. This would be accomplished by freeing ourselves from our ego, which separates us from that power.

"In the thirteenth century, Meister Eckhart said: 'Man must be free in this way, so that he can forget his own self and flow back, with everything he is, into the endless abyss of his origins.' Even if he never used the term, Jesus continually asked us to free ourselves from our egos. I have personally tried everything to achieve that and have only succeeded for a very limited time. The more we try to free ourselves, the more the ego resists, and that explains the failure, for centuries, of the Christians' attempt to make us feel shame. The resistance of the ego is undoubtedly illustrated in the Gospels by the great difficulty the apostles had in applying Jesus's precepts, in awakening the divine that was dormant within themselves. In fact, they hardly ever succeeded, and Jesus lamented this fact all the time, right up until the last evening before his arrest, when he asked them to keep vigil and no one managed it. They all fell asleep, despite their good intentions, which caused Jesus to say: 'The spirit is willing, but the flesh is weak.' But there is a secret."

She paused, and when her voice had stopped echoing throughout the nave, a profound silence filled the entire church.

"There is a secret, and Jesus himself seems to have discovered it toward the end of his life. He repeats it, going so far as to say, at the end, that if there is only one thing to be remembered, it is that. I have only just come to understand that this secret has the power to help us escape the hell of the ego and lead us to a paradise of life awakened. This secret...is to love. When we love, when we feel love, whether it is for a person, an animal, a flower, or a sunset, we are transported beyond ourselves. Our desires, our fears, and our doubts disappear. Our need for affirmation fades away. We no longer seek to compare ourselves

249

to others, to assert our own existence over theirs. Our souls are lifted as we are filled with that feeling, that surge of our hearts, which naturally reaches out to embrace everyone and everything in life. The philosopher Alain said that love is a wondrous urge to leave ourselves. It is also a wondrous urge to find ourselves again, by merging with the universe, with our origins, in a place where our problems no longer exist and where joy reigns."

Alice looked around again at the group of believers. They were listening, but was she truly managing to pass on the message that she knew was essential for happiness and success in life?

"To love means to start by loving yourself. Loving ourselves gives us the strength not to be wounded by the barbs fired by the egos of other people, and not to allow our own egos to react in kind. To love means loving others by managing to see the person behind an ego that is sometimes unpleasant, and thus seeing that ego disappear. To love means finding the strength to love our enemies and transform them into allies. To love means loving life, despite its troubles and difficult blows, and discovering that those are merely tools that allow us to let go, to evolve, to awaken. Love is the key to everything. It is the secret of the world."

Her words echoed throughout the church, beneath the high vaults bathed in sunlight.

She paused and continued with the Mass.

Then she performed the baptism.

# 31

WEDNESDAY, THE END OF THE DAY.

Jeremy was getting ready to leave the confessional, where he was officiating for the last time in Cluny, when he heard the rustling of the curtains on the other side of the thin wooden partition.

As the confessor remained silent, Jeremy invited him to speak. But he said nothing.

"I'm listening," Jeremy said again. "Speak without fear."

He waited patiently, until a woman's voice spoke faintly, a distinguished voice that he recognized without difficulty despite a certain tension.

"Father, I have behaved badly."

She paused for a few seconds. He could hear her breathing through the grating.

"I did something bad, and I feel terrible about it."

Jeremy sometimes heard confessions made in a rather detached tone of voice, and he would wonder if the person was coming out of habit, superstition, or even a simple need to chat. But this voice revealed a feeling of guilt that seemed caused by true suffering.

"I criticized someone ... and that caused him harm."

Jeremy froze. He could feel his heart beating faster, while his mind, usually concentrated on listening, was suddenly troubled by thoughts and emotions. He took a deep breath to get control of himself. Didn't this woman need compassion, in spite of everything? All repentance deserved absolution.

"It did serious harm to him," she said.

He could feel that each word cost her dearly, that she was overwhelmed by remorse.

"Perhaps ..."

"No, not perhaps. Definitely."

Jeremy let out a long sigh. "Who can know?" he whispered. "Epictetus said, 'You will be harmed the moment when you feel you have been harmed.' But to judge a situation, it would be necessary to be carried into the future to have a global vision of the event in question, its true consequences, what it brought with it, what it allowed us to avoid, what it taught us. It is only with distance that we can know all of that."

She remained silent for a long time.

"In any case," she finally blurted out, "I regret the accusations I made. I was unfair and I blame myself."

"God forgives you, my child."

He heard some stifled sobbing.

He quietly added:

"And so do I."

*　　*　　*

"A woman? A woman?"

"Yes, Your Grace," said the curate, a defeated look on his face.

"A woman said Mass!"

The curate sadly closed his eyes and shook his head.

The bishop fell back into his enormous armchair. "A woman. My God, how horrible."

Why had God inflicted such a catastrophe on him? In his own diocese.

The media were sure to latch onto it. All of France would soon know about it. The Holy See as well. He felt he had no strength left, leaving him with just disgust. Such humiliation...

He looked up. The curate, who ordinarily stood so upright in his cassock, seemed to droop, as if crumbling under the weight of events.

"A woman said Mass," the bishop said again, pensively.

"My sources described a sermon that was a pantheistic fusion of religions and that was very far from Catholic doctrine," said the curate in a scornful tone of voice.

The bishop slowly twisted his amethyst ring around his finger. "And you said she baptized the child?"

The curate nodded again.

The bishop sighed.

He should have reacted sooner to the warnings. Listened to his curate. For months he had been asking for sanctions, and he'd been right. That priest and his muse had been defying the bishop's authority for all this time.

He'd waited too long. His patience had prepared the ground for this debacle. His bitterness was all the worse for that.

He looked at his amethyst ring, which he found rather drab. Farewell to the sapphire and purple of the cardinals.

His rancor suddenly turned to anger. He quickly stood up.

"In any case, the baptism is illegal! It is therefore null and void. Strike it from the register and notify the parents. That's one thing sorted out, at least. That cursed priest and his accomplice won't have the last word."

The curate looked up at him.

"I took the liberty of acting before you on that matter, Your Grace, and—"

"You did well."

"And I got some information. According to the code of canonical law, you are correct: the baptism is totally illegal."

"Excellent!"

"It is illegal, but ... valid."

The bishop shot him a terrible look. "What are you talking about?"

"I called Rome, Your Grace. Even though the baptism is illegal, it cannot be made null and void. Canonical law is clear on this: it stands."

★   ★   ★

The young salesman at the Renault dealership was bored stiff that August afternoon. When he heard the soft sound of the automatic door sliding open, he looked up and was surprised to see the Baroness de Sirdegault standing in front of him.

Her old English racing-green Jaguar was parked just outside. With a bit of luck, the old aristocratic lady perhaps wanted to upgrade from coach and horses.

He stood up and walked toward her to welcome her. He was a little nervous, all the same. He didn't have dealings with someone of her rank every day.

"Welcome to the showroom, Madame de Sirdegault."

"Good morning, monsieur," she replied, looking around at the cars.

On the enormous TV screen hanging on the wall, the latest commercial was playing in a loop: at the wheel of a Renault Espace, Kevin Spacey looked straight into the eyes of the viewer while saying: *"I might even be president of the United States."*

He saw his client stop to look over the Captur.

"That car that would be very good for you. It would give you a young, energetic appearance."

She frowned. "Clean your glasses, young man. I'm over sixty," she said with a smile.

He felt as stupid as a child caught doing something wrong.

*Quick. Get control of yourself. Don't dwell on a failure.*

"In that case, the Mégane or even the Talisman would reflect your elegant appearance."

She didn't reply right away, still walking around the cars.

"That's not what I'm looking for," she finally retorted.

He bit his lip. Always the same mistake—he pushed before having the facts. He remembered the advice of the sales trainer: first ask questions, pinpoint the client's image of themselves, which would be reflected by the car of their dreams.

"I see. So tell me everything: what are you looking for?"

She was calmly walking around all the display cars and stopped in front of a used Twingo.

"A car to get me places."

He stood there, dumbstruck. It was the first time someone had told him anything like that. It wasn't normal. He was sure of it— that answer was not in the list of responses in the sales manual. Something wasn't right.

"I need a car," she added, "that will get me to Mâcon once a month to do my shopping."

He had no idea what to say.

She gave him a probing look. "You don't think this one would manage that?"

"Umm…Yes, yes…"

She decided rather quickly to take the car, and a few minutes later, they were sitting in his office to place the order on his computer.

"Please remind me how to spell your name, Madame de Sirdegault."

"It's Gross. Josette Gross. Just as it sounds."

★   ★   ★

Alice got up before dawn. She quickly got dressed, drank some water, and went outside into the dark. The cool air carried the scent of dew, which formed in droplets on the wisteria leaves in front of the house. Down the entire road, the old streetlamps made of burnished bronze spread their dim golden light in the soft half-darkness.

Above the rooftops, very high in the sky, the stars were silently fading away, accompanied by the last crescent of moon, as slender as the blade of a scythe.

At the bottom of the sleepy street, the aroma of bread wafted from the open window of the bakery.

She turned left on the Rue Mercière, then left on the Rue de la Barre, and arrived at the square in front of the church.

A car had stopped, its headlights on, in front of the half-open door of the rectory.

Two clergymen were standing close by, one all in black, the other in purple, his arms crossed. Jeremy's escort to the airport, without a doubt. She would have preferred to arrive before them.

As she got closer, her footsteps echoed on the old paving stones, and the clergyman dressed in black nodded slightly in her direction to point her out. The other man looked her up and down without saying a word, but the expression in his eyes revealed his animosity.

In spite of that, she walked over to them and briefly greeted them as she passed, but got no reply. She reached the door of the church when she saw him.

On the other side of the courtyard, Jeremy was coming down the front steps of the rectory in his black cassock, carrying a small suitcase, the kind of little suitcase a teenager might have, covered in colored stickers. She immediately recognized it, and her heart broke as she recalled the memories of their class trip to Italy, when they were in high school together.

He saw her and walked toward her, smiling.

"You came," he said.

She nodded, too choked up to speak.

They stood for a few seconds, looking at each other without saying a word. Then she took a step toward him and kissed him on the cheek.

"Take care of yourself," she whispered.

He smiled at her reassuringly. Then he started to walk toward the bishop's car.

"I almost forgot," said Alice.

He turned around.

"I saw Madame de Sirdegault last night," she said. "She knew you were going at dawn, and she told me she was leaving a note for you in the sacristy, from someone who couldn't come to meet with you before you left. She didn't say who it was from, but she insisted that you get it before you go."

"In the sacristy? Why in the sacristy?"

"No idea."

He looked at his watch.

"We have to hurry," said the bishop.

Alice and Jeremy looked at each other.

"Come with me," said Jeremy.

Then to the bishop he added: "I'll be right back."

Alice followed him as they quickly walked down the narrow path around the church. They went straight into the sacristy through a narrow door hidden between the buttresses. The door creaked loudly as it opened. Inside, it was dark, with the slight scent of damp incense. Jeremy switched on the wall light.

The envelope was sitting on a small tabernacle. He picked it up and took out a card. On it were simply the handwritten words "Thank you." No signature, no name on the back of the envelope.

Alice suddenly started as she heard the powerful sound of the church organ.

Jeremy opened the door that separated the sacristy from the rest of the church. The lights were on. They went in.

All his faithful flock were there, together, and they stood up when they saw him. The nave was full.

Bach's music filled the church with the poignant chords of "Jesu, Joy of Man's Desiring."

Victor, Étienne, and all the other familiar faces were there, all the faithful who attended Mass and all the people who went to confession. Only one seat was empty. Impossible not to notice as it was in the first row, near the center aisle. No one had dared sit in it.

Alice stepped back so Jeremy could say goodbye to his flock, but he took her hand and they walked forward together.

The parishioners left their seats to join them, surrounding them. They all shook hands, kissed each other on the cheek, spoke words of friendship, gratitude, encouragement, promises to stay in touch one way or another.

One of the parishioners opened the large door. The bishop

and the curate looked very displeased and instinctively moved back into the darkness of the street.

When he got to the end of the center aisle, he saw Madame de Sirdegault sitting in the last row. He hadn't recognized her right away, for her hair wasn't done and she was wearing simple clothing, with no jewelry or makeup. She no longer wore the large gold cross with the big ruby. Despite the tears gathering in her eyes, a new light was shining from within them.

For the first time, he found her beautiful.

Outside, the first rays of light announced the dawning day.

They stepped over the threshold, then Jeremy turned toward his parishioners, looked at them gathered together one last time, and, quoting Jesus, whispered a few words that Alice could barely hear:

"You are the light of the world."